"Wait! WE'RE HERE!!" Sam screamed up at the treetops. "Look down!! Down HERE!" The helicopter hovered for several seconds and then took off again. Now the sound of its blades was getting more and more distant. It disappeared across the valley as it moved to another hillside and hovered there.

"No!" Sara yelled in desperation. "Come back!"

Sam's face was white with fear. He was so stunned by what had just happened that he didn't even notice the blood streaming from his arm down onto his jeans and shoes.

"This isn't good," he choked out. He'd been trying to stay brave for the sake of Sara, but this was just too much. "They . . . they think we're not here."

LOST ON THE MOUNTAIN

MARK THOMAS

Lost on the Mountain

TP THE TOWNSEND LIBRARY

For more titles in the Townsend Library,
visit our website: **www.townsendpress.com**

Townsend Press, Inc.
439 Kelley Drive
West Berlin, NJ 08091
permissions@townsendpress.com

ISBN: 978-1-59194-305-1

Library of Congress Control Number:
2013933068

CHAPTER 1

"It's not fair!"

Sam Brooks shouted out angrily into the evening sky. He threw a fistful of rocks as hard as he could. They spun out into the air and then dropped soundlessly for nearly 1,000 feet. Sam could barely hear a small clattering far below as the rocks struck a mountain ledge. It was eerie. What if he hadn't noticed the way the grass suddenly disappeared and the air became cooler? He would have walked right off the ledge and fallen into nothingness—and to his death.

His sister, Sara, sat huddled beneath a tall pine tree trying not to cry. Her legs were scratched from walking through bushes and prickly vines, and both knees were bleeding from slipping on sharp rocks. The sky was quickly growing dark, and strange scurrying sounds were coming from the woods.

1

"What are we going to do, Sam?" Sara kept asking.

Sam just shook his head.

"What if it gets cold? What if there are . . . bears? What if . . ."

"I don't know!" Sam finally yelled. Then he turned back to Sara and took a deep breath.

"I know this doesn't look good," he finally said quietly. "But I'll figure out something to do. We're going to be okay. I promise."

Sam paced toward the cliff and then quickly stepped back. The sharp drop made his stomach feel funny. Off in the distance, dark rainclouds were growing. Every now and then, streaks of chain lightning darted across the sky, followed by low, faraway thunder. It sounded like a threat, a quiet warning. Something bad was coming. Something very bad.

Sam crouched down and put his head in his hands. He had to think. What *was* he going to do? And how had everything gone so terribly wrong? How on earth had they ended up here?

Think back, Sam murmured to himself. *Retrace everything, every detail.*

Sam had a vague memory of a TV show about a teenage boy who had gotten lost at sea when trying to sail alone across the Pacific

Ocean. The boy explained that by very carefully going through all his memories from the past few weeks, he was able to figure out what had gone wrong. At the time, Sam thought it was ridiculous.

"Yeah, right," Sam had said with a laugh. "Like some kid could really find his way out of a 12,000-mile-wide ocean by thinking about what he had eaten for lunch a week earlier."

But now it didn't seem so funny. Maybe details were important. And anyway, pacing and panicking and yelling surely weren't going to help the situation. So Sam closed his eyes and thought. Surely, he did not need to think back three weeks—he couldn't even if he wanted to. Maybe three or four days ago would work.

About three days ago, I was . . .

In spite of his fear and worry, Sam almost smiled. Had he really also shouted that things weren't fair just this past Sunday evening?

"It's not fair! If I don't want to go, I shouldn't have to go."

Sam stood with his arms folded, glaring at his mother. His shaggy brown hair kept falling into his eyes, and he pushed it back angrily.

"What is wrong with you, Sam?" his mother asked, sounding more irritated than concerned. "This is exactly the kind of thing you always say you want to do—hiking and adventure and stuff. Plus, it'll be a good way to meet some of the kids at your new school before the school year begins."

"I don't want to meet anyone else here," Sam grumbled. "They're all a bunch of hicks. This whole town is a waste of my time."

"Excuse me?" Sam's mother said, half angrily and half jokingly. "This is where I grew up, young man. So I'd watch it if I were you."

Sam just shrugged and turned away quickly from his mother's stare. He rubbed a painful knot just above his left cheekbone.

"We can talk about it some more during lunch, but you're going regardless of how you feel about this town," his mother said. "And change your shirt. You look like you've been rolling around in the dirt or something."

Sam stomped to his room and slammed the door. He flung himself down on his bed and stared at the ceiling for a full ten minutes. Then he picked up the brochure and read it again:

Seven wonderful days in the Blue Ridge Mountains at Camp Crystal! In exchange for working on the trails, young people (ages 10-15) will enjoy hiking, camping, swimming at Crystal Lake, and nightly cookouts and campfires. This terrific opportunity fills up quickly every year, so sign up now!

Sam looked at the pictures on the brochure. They showed kids around his age clearing trails with shovels and rakes. On the opposite side of the page, kids were splashing in a blue mountain lake. They looked equally thrilled to be doing either activity. The first time Sam had seen the brochure, he thought it looked like it might be a lot of fun. But now those pictures made Sam roll his eyes. He wadded the brochure into a ball and hurled it across the room. It landed on top of a pile of books that Sam needed for his classes when school started in two weeks.

Only two weeks! Sam thought miserably. He would be a freshman at Washington High School in the small town of Blueville, North Carolina—*if* he lived through the stupid trip to the mountains. For nearly three years, Sam had practically been counting the days until he would finally be in high school. But that was back home in Washington, D.C. Now, suddenly, everything had changed. Sam's stepfather, Don, had gotten into some kind of trouble that Sam's mother wouldn't completely explain.

"There's no reason for you to know about all that," his mother had said. "Too many boring details."

But Sam knew enough to figure out that it probably had something to do with his stepfather's drinking too much and losing his temper. It happened all the time. Usually, Don just yelled and maybe kicked a door or broke something. But other times he would hit Sam. Sam didn't like being punched and slapped by a grown man, but he could stand it if he just shut his eyes and pretended he was somewhere else. What he couldn't stand was watching Don hit his sister or his mother.

Sometimes Sam lay awake at night imagining being big enough to fight back. If he weren't so small, he'd smack Don so hard in the face that he'd never mess with him again—much less with Sara or his mother. But Sam was the smallest 14-year-old boy in his school. It was something that his stepfather never missed an opportunity to point out.

"I could snap your arm like a twig," Don had drunkenly sneered one time as he yanked Sam's arm. "There are 10-year-old *girls* that could punch you out! Man, you are the littlest and most useless excuse for a boy that I've ever seen."

Several times, Sam's mother had taken him and his sister to a cheap hotel for a few days to get away from Don.

"Why don't we just leave for good?" Sam asked whenever it got that bad. He couldn't understand how his mother could bear being around someone like that. Sam didn't remember his real father, but he knew there was no way he could have been as awful as his stepfather.

But Sam's mother just shook her head and said, "We can't do that."

"Why not?" Sam would demand angrily. "We could just pack up and leave and go somewhere where he'd never find us!"

Then Sam's mother would look very tired and put her arm around Sam and sigh.

"No, Sam. You don't understand," she'd say. "I just can't do that. It's not that simple, and it's not going to happen."

But now, it *had* happened.

In the middle of the night, two months earlier, Sam had awakened to some frantic shouting, a slamming door, and the sound of breaking glass. Then flashing blue lights lit up his bedroom wall, and voices on the street, three stories below, grew louder. Sam ran to his window and strained to see what was happening, but he caught only a glimpse of a police officer putting someone in handcuffs in the back seat of a squad car. Was it Don? Sam dashed out into the hallway and called for his mother, but there was no answer. The front door to their apartment was wide open.

Sam began sprinting down the stairs in his bare feet. There were broken beer bottles strewn on the stairs, which Sam had to hop over. When he was halfway down, his mother came around the corner. On her cheek was an ugly red scratch that dripped blood down to her jaw. Sam could tell that she had been crying. In her hand was something that looked like an official form. When she saw Sam looking at it, she shoved it in a back pocket. Then she put her hand out and pointed back upstairs.

"Start packing" was all she said.

The next day, Sam, his sister, and their mother were crammed into their old beat-up Honda, headed to North Carolina. Their mother's brother, Joe, said they were welcome to stay with him as long as they needed.

"Do you think Uncle Joe will get sick of us and kick us out in a few days?" Sara whispered. "And then we'll have nowhere to go?"

Sara and Sam were sitting close together in the back seat, since the front seat was piled with boxes and clothes and maps.

"What?" Sam said, looking at Sara. Her lip was quivering, and tears brimmed in her eyes. Immediately, Sam reached over and put his arm around his 10-year-old sister. Sara was small like Sam, and she had been born with one leg a little shorter than the other, so she limped and couldn't run very fast. Sometimes kids made fun of her. Sam knew what that felt like.

"No. Of course not," Sam said quietly. "Uncle Joe's not some jerk like Don—you know that. He's always been great when he's come to visit us. Remember that time he brought you that 6-foot kite? "

Sara just snuffled and looked out the window. Sam handed her a piece of a candy bar he was eating. Other boys his age generally ignored their sisters, but Sam was different. Since the first time he had seen his stepfather slap Sara, Sam knew he needed to watch out for his younger sister. Whenever Don hit Sara, Sam sat with her in her bedroom until she fell asleep, sometimes telling her old stories to calm her down. Maybe he wasn't very big. Maybe things weren't fair. But he could protect Sara.

"Everything's going to turn out okay," Sam said.

Up ahead, towering mountains covered in a bluish mist came into view. Sam had never seen anything like them outside of movies and magazines. They rose up into the sky like dark thunderclouds coming out of the ground. With every mile, the mountains got taller and taller. Their sheer size made Sam feel frightened in a creepy way. And worse than that, they made him feel smaller than he'd ever felt before.

CHAPTER 2

"You've got to be kidding!"

Sam stood in his uncle's kitchen. They had been at Uncle Joe's for a week and a half now. Sam was staring at his mother with a stunned expression.

"No," his mother said. "I'm not kidding. Look, Sam, it's not that big of a deal. You'll get used to it."

"Not that big of a deal?" Sam said as his voice cracked. "It's a huge deal! I thought we were going to be here only a few weeks, tops. And now, like all of a sudden, you decide we're going to stay here *permanently*?"

His mother sighed.

"It's not all of a sudden. You know I've started looking for a job. And anyway, I thought you liked it here. I thought this would be exciting news. Haven't you already made some new friends? What are their names—Bart and Alex?"

Sam frowned and turned away from his mother. She was right. Sort of. Sam had liked it in Blueville when they first arrived. They were 400 miles away from Don. It was exciting to be somewhere new and different for a while, and he had met two older boys from a couple blocks away who had been friendly—at first. Bart and Alex were both 17, loud, and in charge of their neighborhood and beyond. Bart even owned a shiny black Jeep, a present his father had given him as soon as he was old enough to drive. Whenever Bart drove it, he gunned the engine loudly so everyone would look at him.

Alex lived two houses down from Bart. He didn't own a car, but he was tall and played both football and basketball for the nearby high school's teams. He even had a half-grown moustache and a girlfriend. Sam couldn't believe it when the two of them pulled up in front of his uncle's house one afternoon. Sam had just been sitting on the porch, staring into space when he was startled by the roar of the Jeep.

"Hey dude!" Alex shouted. "You live here now?"

Sam looked around at first to see who Alex was talking to. Older kids, particularly ones who owned cars, never talked to Sam.

"Uh, sort of," Sam said. "We're visiting my uncle."

"Oh, yeah. Your uncle is that weird old guy that lives alone and fiddles around with toilets all day," Bart snorted from the driver's seat.

"Well, he's . . . he's a plumber," Sam said awkwardly. It was true that Uncle Joe lived alone, but he wasn't weird. He was just kind of quiet and kept to himself. But he was one of the nicest people Sam had ever known. Uncle Joe came to D.C. every year during the summer for a visit, and he always brought really excellent presents.

"Whatever," Alex said. Then he turned to Bart, and they talked quietly for a few minutes. "We're going to the batting cages up at our high school to hit some balls. You wanna go?" he finally said to Sam.

Sam couldn't believe it.

"I . . . I have to ask my mom," Sam sputtered.

Bart and Alex snickered at this, but they waited until Sam came flying back outside. His mother just stood on the porch and waved.

Sam had begged her not to come out and ask Bart and Alex a million questions.

"They're just high school kids like me," Sam had said in a hurry. Then he added with a note of pride, "And they want to hang out."

That afternoon, Sam had a pretty good time with his new friends, even though he couldn't understand why they kept laughing at things he said that weren't supposed to be funny. And the things he said that he thought *were* pretty funny, they just ignored. But Bart and Alex didn't make fun of how Sam missed nearly every ball that was pitched to him. And when they found out he was 14, they didn't make any of the typical, "But you're so *little*!" comments he usually heard. They even paid for a milkshake on the way home.

The next day, Bart and Alex invited Sam over to Bart's house to play video games while his parents were at work. Bart turned up the music extra loud and pulled a pile of food out of the refrigerator for everyone to eat.

"Man, you are lucky to be able to just be here alone and do whatever you want," Sam said as he shoveled in handfuls of M&Ms.

"Yeah," Alex said, grinning and smoothing his patchy moustache. "Bart and I are a little old for babysitters."

"Oh, I don't have a babysitter either," Sam said quickly. "I mean, I have to look after my sister."

The fact was that, until just six months ago, an elderly next-door neighbor had looked after Sam and Sara when their mother and stepfather weren't home.

"Sisters. Ugh," Alex said with disgust. "What a pain. I have a 10-year-old sister that I stay away from as much as possible. There's no *way* I'm spending my time looking after her. My parents know better than to even ask me."

"Your sister is 10?" Sam asked thoughtfully. "Maybe she and my sister could—"

But Sam was cut off by Bart's whooping and walking back into the room from the kitchen again. In his hands were three bottles.

"It's happy hour, boys!" he announced loudly, plunking the bottles down on the table. "You like beer, don't you, Sam?"

Bart and Alex both took huge swigs and then looked at Sam. Sam just sat and stared at his bottle uncomfortably.

"Come on, man," Alex said. "I thought you were from the big city. You and your friends must party all the time there. Drink up!"

Sam picked up the bottle and then put it down again.

"It's . . . it's just that I'm, you know, not thirsty right now," he said nervously.

Alex and Bart burst into loud laughter. "Hey, breaking news, Sam. No one drinks beer because they're *thirsty*," Bart scoffed.

"How'd you buy beer if you're only 17?" Sam asked, trying to take the attention away from himself.

Bart finished his bottle in four big gulps, burped loudly, and high-fived Alex.

"This is my parents' stuff," Bart said as he stood up to get another one. "They never miss it if I only take a few."

"But it's pretty easy to buy beer. Or, at least, it used to be," Alex said. Then he and Bart looked at each other and grinned.

"Yeah, Sam, that was something we were going to ask you about," Bart said as he twisted off a cap. "You'll help your buddies get some beer, won't you?"

"What?" Sam asked blankly.

"You know," Alex said casually. "Ask some old guy walking into a convenience store to buy it for you. Tell him a sob story like your mom sent you because she has a broken leg or something. Tell him he can keep the change."

"We'd do it ourselves," Bart added quickly, "except that we're too old now. It'd look suspicious."

Sam just sat and nodded and didn't say anything. After putting up with the drunken rages of his stepfather, he didn't want to have anything to do with alcohol. And he sure wasn't about to break the law for two guys he barely knew. But at the same time, he felt pretty cool having older friends. He didn't want to lose them. He just kept nodding.

"Great!" Bart said, and gave Sam a friendly slap on the back. "I knew you were all right."

Then Bart and Alex went back to the video game and dropped the subject. *Maybe they'll just forget about it*, Sam thought hopefully. *Maybe they were just kidding*.

When Sam saw Bart and Alex two days later, they didn't mention anything about getting beer. Sam was relieved and figured it had all been a joke. Sometimes he didn't get their sense of humor, but he figured it was just because Bart and Alex were older. But the very next day, a Friday, Sam discovered it had not been a joke at all.

"Okay, Sam. It's time for you to do some

acting," Bart said with a grin as he pulled into a convenience store parking lot. "Hey— look at that old homeless-looking geezer over there. Perfect! Here's twenty bucks. Tell him mommy needs three six-packs. He can keep whatever change is left over."

Sam's face turned pale. "Huh? I . . . I thought we were going to a baseball game," Sam stammered.

"Yeah," Alex said impatiently. "We're going with beer. And with enough beer left over for some more fun tonight. Get going, kid."

Sam froze. Both Alex and Bart were looking at him with expressions that were rapidly changing from friendly to dangerous. It reminded Sam of a movie he had recently seen about vampires. Bart's smile turned to a threat. Alex smoothed his moustache with a hand that turned into a fist.

"What's your problem?" Bart hissed. "Move it!"

"I don't think . . . I can't . . . ," Sam stammered. "It's not right."

"Not *right*?" Bart growled as he shoved the twenty-dollar bill into Sam's face. "I'll show you what's not right if you don't get moving."

"After everything we've done for you," Alex said, glaring at Sam. "Like anyone else would hang out with some little sissy that looks like a third-grader!"

Now Sam was really frightened. He realized in a flash that he had been tricked. Alex and Bart's friendship had, in fact, been a joke that he hadn't gotten at all.

"I'll just go home . . . I can't . . . ," Sam barely whispered as he reached for the car door.

Instantly, Alex's fist slammed into his shoulder and threw him back against the car seat. Then he grabbed Sam by the collar, shook him roughly, and punched the side of his head so hard that Sam saw tiny stars for a few seconds.

"Get out of my car," Bart yelled. "And we better not ever see your sorry coward face again, or you're gonna get it way worse than this."

Sam stumbled out of the car and stood in the parking lot in a daze as the black Jeep roared away. He rubbed the side of his head and began walking the two miles back to his uncle's house. Once Sam's fear faded, it was replaced by anger—mostly at himself.

I can't do anything right! Sam fumed. *I'm too small to stand up to anyone or anything! And I'm too stupid to realize when someone's using me.*

Sam's only comfort was in knowing that this visit to Blueville was temporary. Before long, he'd be back in D.C. Sure, Don would be there, but hopefully his mother wouldn't have anything to do with that loser again. And Sam's friends, his *real* friends, would be there. Maybe they didn't have cars or play on a football team, but they liked Sam for who he was. They got all his jokes and never made him feel scared.

Deep in the middle of these thoughts, Sam wandered into his uncle's kitchen, where his mother gave him the "exciting" news about staying in Blueville permanently. Sam slumped into a chair and rubbed his head while his mother started making dinner. From down the hallway came shrieks of laughter, endless giggling, and a girl's voice that Sam didn't recognize.

"Who's here?" Sam asked dully.

"Oh," his mother said, "that's Vicky, the girl from two blocks over—Alex's sister. She's staying for dinner."

Sam felt a pang of fear rush through him.

"Which reminds me," his mother added. "Alex is coming by to pick her up afterwards. It'll be nice to finally meet him. Make sure to invite him in and introduce him."

CHAPTER 3

Sam avoided Alex that evening by pretending to feel sick even before dinner began. In fact, he did feel kind of sick and shaky knowing that Alex was coming over. Sam hid in his room, leafing through a pile of old adventure magazines he had brought with him. His favorite was one called *Real Survival*. It was full of true stories about people who had climbed brutal mountains, battled monster seas, and hiked through burning deserts—and lived to tell about it. Sam loved reading about fearless people who seemed to enjoy looking danger right in the eye.

"I wish I could be like that," Sam grumbled to himself. "But I'm too scared to even come out of my *room*!"

For the next several days, Sam did everything he could to steer clear of being seen by Alex and Bart. He didn't wander over to the nearby park to watch baseball games, even though he wanted to. He turned down an offer from Uncle Joe to spend an afternoon at a local swimming pool, because he had once heard Bart talk about having had fun at that pool. And now when Sam sat on the front porch, he jumped up and dashed inside whenever he heard the loud roar of a car engine headed his way.

"What in the world are you doing?" his mother asked when she saw him scurry inside and hide behind the door for the third time in an hour.

Sam just shrugged and looked away. There was no way he wanted his mom to know what was going on. He was sure that she would march right over to Alex's and Bart's homes and complain to their parents. Then he'd *really* be in trouble.

"There's a wasp or something flying around," Sam said. "It was . . . uh . . . scaring me."

His mother just looked at him and shook her head.

"Well, I've never known you to be afraid of bugs before," she said. "And I hope it's not going to keep you from wanting to do this."

Sam's mother handed him the brochure about the week in the mountains. He looked it over for a long time. Then he smiled.

"Wow," Sam finally said. "That sounds pretty cool, actually."

Then he paused as he looked at the description again.

"So . . . so kids older than 15 can't go?" he asked nervously. "It's only for 10- to 14-year-olds?"

"No one over 15 allowed," his mother said. "I figured you'd be hoping those two older boys could go, but this will be a good way for you to meet some of the kids your own age who will be in your class."

Sam pretended to be a little disappointed, but then he said, "Sounds good to me."

"Sara will be going, too. But since her new friend, Vicky, will also be there, she shouldn't bother you too much."

Sam felt a quick sting of panic.

"But Vicky's brother isn't going, right?" he asked with wide eyes.

"No, Sam," his mother said somewhat impatiently. "I told you—he's too old. I'm sure you can still have a good time there without those two boys."

"Oh, I'm sure I can," Sam said, hiding a grin of relief.

For the rest of the week, Sam filled his time by reading about the Blue Ridge Mountains and planning for the trip. Uncle Joe had loads of books about the trails, wildlife, and history of the mountains. Sam couldn't believe that the rocks that made the mountains were billions of years old, or that wild pigs with sharp tusks roamed parts of the mountain range. Hundreds of trails wove through the hills, including the Appalachian Trail, which was more than 2,000 miles long! Still, most of the mountains were wild and pretty desolate. Again and again, the books warned hikers not to wander away from the trails and into the woods.

"Hey, did you know that where we're going, there's a ghost that haunts the woods?" Sam said to Sara at dinner three nights before the trip. "I read about it in one of Uncle Joe's books."

Uncle Joe just smiled and nodded at his nephew.

"Don't scare your sister," their mom said, passing a bowl of green beans.

"As if I'd be scared," Sara said with a huff. "Geez, Mom. I'm not a baby. I know ghosts aren't real."

"Oh, but this one might be," Uncle Joe said playfully. "About a hundred years ago, Old Man Smith was bullied off his land by two brothers. The two men took over his farm and cabin. The legend goes that Smith died not long after that. But then he kept coming back to haunt those brothers. Maybe he's looking for revenge, or maybe he's just angry. No one knows for sure."

"Yeah," Sam said excitedly. "And lots of people say they've seen an old-timey sort of guy wandering around near where Smith's cabin used to be—and also up near Camp Crystal."

Sara looked only slightly nervous.

"Well, even if that *were* true, he doesn't sound like a scary ghost," she said. "He was just mad at those two bullies. He wouldn't bother anyone today."

Sam just shrugged.

"Maybe so," he said mysteriously. "All I know is that if I have to get up in the middle of the night to go to the bathroom or something at this camp, I don't want to see some ancient ghost dude walking toward me and—"

"Okay, that's enough," Mom said.

Sara giggled, and Sam winked at her. "She knows I'm kidding, Mom."

The next morning, Uncle Joe asked Sam if he'd go to the hardware store a mile or so away and pick up a latch he needed for the basement door.

"You can borrow my bike," Uncle Joe said. "I think if we lower the seat a bit, it should be fine. Then you can ride it as much as you want. I'm sorry to say, it's been quite a while since I've been out on my bike, um, exercising."

Uncle Joe pointed at his rather large stomach and sighed dramatically.

For a moment, Sam worried that Alex or Bart might see him. But it had been more than a week now. Maybe they weren't mad anymore. Plus, what would they be doing at a hardware store? Bart had once bragged that he hadn't made his bed in 8 months. They definitely wouldn't be shopping for things to help their parents fix up their homes.

"Sure. Thanks, Uncle Joe," Sam said. "Anything else you want me to pick up?"

"Why don't you get some heavy-duty trash bags," Uncle Joe said, handing Sam some money. "I'll show you how to use them to keep yourself dry if it rains when you're hiking."

Once the seat was lowered, Sam jumped on the bike and took off. It felt great to be out of the house for a change—and unafraid. The late Saturday morning was warm and sunny, and it seemed like everyone was out doing something. On the way to the hardware store, Sam passed his new high school. His mom had gone to that exact same school twenty years earlier. It was an old brick building surrounded by tall oak trees and flowering bushes. Several boys his age were throwing around a football in one of the fields while some girls watched.

It might be okay, Sam thought, hopefully. He missed his old friends back in D.C., but at least he was going to be a freshman, so it would be a new start for everyone in his class. And Bart and Alex would be seniors. Surely they wouldn't waste their time picking on a lowly freshman, Sam figured. And several other incoming freshmen were going on this trip, so Sam might even make some new friends before school began. Maybe even a girlfriend! Suddenly, Sam felt foolish for having let Bart and Alex upset him so much. Probably they had already completely forgotten about him.

Inspired by these positive thoughts, Sam raced down the long hill to the hardware store. Before picking up the latch and bags, Sam wandered over to a section that had some things for hikers. This was pretty unusual for a hardware store, but since the store was right in the middle of the mountains and not far from some major trails, it stocked a handful of necessities. Sam picked up a compass and fiddled with it, figuring out the direction of Uncle Joe's house by lining up the arrows. He'd never had to use a compass before. But he'd read about them again and again in *Real Survival* magazines. It was pretty cool to see how one actually worked.

By the time Sam finally got the bags and latch, he realized he'd been in the hardware store for nearly an hour.

"You a fan of hiking?" the woman who rang up the purchases asked Sam. When Sam explained that he'd never been on a hike, but was going on a 7-day trip starting Monday, the woman nodded.

"Ah, Camp Crystal," she said with a smile. "You'll have a great time. This is the third year my daughter's gone—Deanna is her name. Maybe you'll meet her."

Sam felt a little embarrassed and just nodded.

"But watch out for that ghost!" the woman, with a grin, called after Sam as he was leaving. Sam turned back and smiled with a slight roll of his eyes to let her know that he wasn't afraid.

Not afraid, Sam thought as he pushed open the door. *And that's the way it's gonna stay.* As he was counting his change and wondering if he should get some ice cream, he heard it—a voice that made all his bravery evaporate suddenly and completely.

"Well, well, well. If it isn't little Sammy."

Bart was leaning against the wall of the store, smoking a cigarette. Alex was sitting on the crossbar of Uncle Joe's bike with his arms crossed. When Sam stopped in his tracks, both of them laughed nastily, and Bart flicked his cigarette at Sam. It bounced off his knee in a shower of sparks.

"I thought we told you we didn't want to see you again," Bart said, as he straightened up and began moving toward Sam. "I thought we told you what was gonna happen if you didn't stay out of our way, you little jerk."

Sam tried to speak, but he couldn't. His mouth had gone dry and his heart was racing. Finally, he just pointed to the bike and stammered, "That's my bike. I . . . I'll just . . . I mean, I was just leaving."

Bart motioned to the bike. "Go ahead, then. Get on your bike and leave."

Alex was still sitting on the bike. Now he grinned.

"Yeah, come and get it."

Sam was trapped. Not knowing what else to do, he stepped toward the bike. In a flash, Bart grabbed Sam by his shirt and spun him around. Bart's face was so close that Sam could feel him spitting when he talked.

"Man, you are in the wrong place at the wrong time," Bart growled. "You're in for a world of hurt."

CHAPTER 4

For one horrifying moment, Sam thought he was going to start crying. But he knew it would only make things worse. So instead, he lowered his head and blocked his face, both for protection and to hide his fear. When he heard Bart and Alex laughing at him, he looked up. Instantly, Alex raised his fist, and Sam flinched.

"You are pathetic," Alex said, still laughing. Bart jumped at Sam, and Sam quickly cowered and covered his head again with both hands. At this, Bart nearly doubled over with loud laughter.

"Look, his hands are shaking," Alex pointed out to Bart. Then he turned back to Sam. "Dude, don't wet your pants or anything. Man, my 10-year-old sister is braver than you! Bigger, too."

Sam just folded his arms and stared at the ground, waiting for whatever was going to happen to happen. He hated himself for being so afraid and so small—almost more than he hated Bart and Alex at that very moment. But at least he wasn't going to run away or beg them to leave him alone. He wouldn't give them that much satisfaction.

Just then, a man and his daughter walked by and stared at the three boys.

"Everything okay here?" he asked when he noticed Sam's frightened face.

"Oh, sure," Alex said innocently. "Just teaching my little brother here how to ride a bike, and he's kind of scared. You know how kids are."

Bart snickered. Sam felt more humiliated than he could ever remember feeling. He hoped the man could see that he was obviously too old to be learning how to ride a bike. But to Sam's further embarrassment, the man just smiled and nodded. "Good luck!" he said, and disappeared around the corner.

Bart and Alex burst out laughing again. Then Bart took a quick look around and gave Sam a sudden hard shove. Sam fell to the ground, dropping the bag with the latch in it. When he scrambled to get back up, Alex casually stepped over and gave Sam a heavy kick in the side. It knocked the wind out of him. As Sam was struggling for breath, Bart looked around again and picked up the bag.

"Don't forget this, errand boy," Bart said, and threw the bag toward Sam. The metal latch hit Sam just above his left cheekbone. At first Sam was stunned, and then he felt a burning, spreading pain. He grabbed at his face, expecting to find blood, but all he found was a painful lump that was already growing. He hunched over on the ground, protecting his face with his hands and breathing in quick gasps.

"Well, we'll see you around, *Samantha*," Bart said. He and Alex both had a good laugh at that one.

"Oh, and by the way, my sister told me that you're going to be at that lame camp for losers next week," Alex said. "We've had some pretty good times driving up there in the middle of the night and scaring all the losers, haven't we Bart?"

Bart nodded and broke into a wide, mean grin. "Definitely. Good times. Yeah, we may be seeing you pretty soon, Samantha."

With that, Bart and Alex walked off. Sam waited until he heard the roar of Bart's Jeep fade before he got on the bike. Slowly and painfully, he pedaled back up the hill. *No way*, he thought bitterly. *There is no way I'm going to that camp now and have those two jerks make a fool of me in front of everyone before school even starts.*

As soon as he got back to Uncle Joe's house, Sam walked through the kitchen and told his mother that he'd changed his mind. He definitely wasn't going to Camp Crystal.

"You have to go," his mother said without even turning around from making sandwiches on the counter. "Your uncle and I are using that week to go back to D.C. and pack up everything in the apartment and move it down here."

"It's not fair!" Sam said desperately. "If I don't want to go, I shouldn't have to go!"

Come Monday morning, however, Sam and Sara were on a rattling old school bus with about sixty other kids on their way to the camp. Sam sat looking out the window with his face turned so that the dark bruise on his face wasn't so noticeable. When his mother asked what had happened, Sam just said he'd had a little bike accident, and left it at that.

Three seats behind him, Sara and Vicky were chattering excitedly. Sam was glad his sister had made such a good friend, but it bothered him that Vicky's brother was one of his worst enemies. Suddenly, Sam missed home back in D.C. intensely. He'd hated living with Don, but at least he'd had friends he could escape with now and then. Now, he had no one and no escape. And all the laughter and noise on the bus didn't make things any better.

Everyone fits in but me, Sam thought bitterly. *Maybe Don was right. Maybe I am just a useless excuse for a human being.*

As these gloomy thoughts filled Sam's mind, the bus began climbing a tall mountain. Thick, green forest sloped up one side, and through his window, Sam could catch glimpses of the valley getting smaller and smaller down below. Sam had never been in an airplane, but he imagined that this must feel kind of like flying. In spite of his gloom, Sam began getting a little excited. Every mile or so, wooden signs pointed out trailheads. Now and then, hikers appeared through the trees.

A group of four boys, maybe only a few years older than Sam, were resting near a trailhead, their huge backpacks on the ground. Two of the boys smiled and waved as the bus roared by. A group of older girls near the back of the bus burst into giggles and shrieks.

"Wow, we're getting pretty high up here."

A boy with wide eyes and a lot of freckles had moved across the aisle of the bus so he could look out Sam's window. He was eating chips from a bag and had a layer of crumbs down the front of his shirt.

"Yeah," Sam replied. "I hope there's a net down there big enough to catch a bus."

The boy, who introduced himself as Pete, laughed and ate another handful of chips.

"Want some?" he asked, offering Sam the bag. Sam took a few and glanced at Pete's shirt and pointed.

"Saving some for a snack later?" Sam asked with a grin. Pete laughed again but didn't bother brushing off his shirt.

"Hey, which cabin are you in?" Pete asked.

"Cabin?" Sam said blankly.

"You know—Arrow, Hilltop, Pine . . . ," Pete said. "They put us in cabins based on our ages."

"Boys and girls together?" Sam asked with a fake look of innocence. At this, Pete really laughed loudly and hit the back of the seat in front of him, making a pretty girl with green eyes pop her head over the seat and pretend to glare at Pete.

"Oh. Excuse me, Deanna," Pete said in a super-sweet voice.

"You're not excused," Deanna chirped. Then she looked at Sam, smiled quickly, and said "hi" before disappearing behind her seat again. Pete just laughed and shook his head.

"Hey, is that the girl whose mom works at the hardware store?" Sam asked in a low voice.

Pete nodded. "Did you just move here or something? Everyone knows the Wilsons. Deanna's older brother, Adam, is the quarterback at Washington High."

Sam frowned slightly. "Yeah, we moved here just a few weeks ago. Is he Deanna's brother? Is he . . . friends with two guys named Bart and Alex?"

"No way," Pete said as he crammed more chips in his mouth and looked out the window at the steep drop. "Those guys are total jerks. They're always getting in trouble and picking fights and stuff. It's a good thing they like each other, 'cause no one else can stand them."

Somehow, this made Sam feel a lot better.

"Ouch," Pete suddenly said, staring at Sam. "What happened to your face?"

For a moment, Sam considered telling Pete everything. Instead, he just mumbled, "Bike wreck," and quickly began rooting around in his backpack and pulled out a piece of paper.

"Arrow," Sam said, reading from a list. "I'm in Arrow."

"Cool!" Pete said. "Me, too. So are you a freshman at Washington this fall, too?"

"Yep," Sam said, relieved that someone his age thought he was the same age. "Only two weeks away. Wow."

"Well, at least you'll get to meet some of the guys in our class on this trip," Pete said. Then he added, "And some of the *girls*." He raised his voice and kicked the back of Deanna's seat again. Sam heard her and another girl laugh. One of them threw a wadded-up candy bar wrapper over the seat. It bounced off Pete's head, leaving crumbled chocolate sprinkled on his face.

"Hey!" he said, and tossed a chip in Deanna's direction.

Sam grinned and looked back out the window at the endless green mountains and streaming sunlight. Blueville, far down in the valley, seemed like it was a million miles away.

Maybe this trip won't be so bad after all, Sam thought to himself.

CHAPTER 5

"**S**o, the two things you need to always remember are never taunt or feed any of the wild animals, and never *ever* wander off a trail into the woods alone."

All of the Camp Crystal participants were gathered in a big picnic shelter listening to the camp director, Shirley. Shirley told everyone to call her by her first name, but Sam couldn't imagine doing that. She was older than his mother. Plus, she was rather stern, knew a million facts and figures about the mountains, and wore a green park ranger's uniform with a very starched collar.

"Can we wander off the trail with someone else?" a tall boy with a goofy grin asked as he looked around the shelter and winked at one of the girls. Nearly everyone laughed. Even Shirley managed a tight smile, but then she was all business again.

"Let me tell you a brief story about two young people who decided to take a little, shall we say, side trip during a hike."

Shirley went on to tell about two teens who'd been on a group trip similar to theirs. One afternoon, during a 10-mile day hike, the two disappeared from the group. They had been near the back of the long line of hikers. Apparently, they'd said something about needing to stop and tie their shoes. Those in front of them just kept hiking and didn't think much about it. After all, how long could it take to tie a shoe?

"No one realized they were missing for quite a while," Shirley said to the hushed group. "Everyone called for them and backtracked for a couple miles. But there was no trace of the two teens. By the time search crews were assembled, it was already getting dark—too dark to search."

Everyone in the shelter was absolutely quiet.

"Did they . . . did they have to spend the night alone in the woods?" Sara asked in a small voice. Sam looked over at her. Sara did not exactly like speaking up in a crowd, but she seemed completely absorbed by Shirley's story.

Her forehead was bunched up with worry, and she was tapping her foot nervously.

"Yes, indeed, they did," Shirley said, looking around and folding her arms.

"So, wow. Were they, like, totally freaked out or something when the rescuers found them?" asked an older girl with braces, who was sitting right up front.

"Oh, I'm sure they were, as you say, freaked out," Shirley continued. "But they were never found—not alive, anyway."

There was a little "oh!" from some of the girls in the back of the shelter.

"Weeks later, only three miles away from the trail they had been on, some hikers came across the boy's jacket, one of the girl's shoes, and both her socks," Shirley said. "Searchers figured the two had gotten turned around, and when they realized they were lost, they panicked and began running. Then they *really* got lost."

There was a long silence in the shelter. Then a small boy sitting next to the girl with braces asked, "Why did that girl take off her socks?"

"That's a good question," Shirley said. "Do any of you know what hypothermia is?"

There were some shouts of "when you freeze" and "too cold." Shirley nodded.

"The night these two young people got lost, temperatures dipped below freezing up in the mountains. There's a very good chance they never made it through the night, wearing only light jackets," Shirley explained. "And in the last stages of hypothermia, something goes haywire, and victims begin to feel hot instead of cold. That's probably why those hikers found a discarded jacket and shoes."

"So . . . so they just died from being too cold?" the small boy asked. "Not from bears?"

There was some snickering in the shelter, but Shirley nodded.

"Most people who get lost in the wilderness die from hypothermia," she said. "And up here, it's possible to get too cold even in the middle of the summer. On that note, I should also tell you that the third thing to remember is to always carry protection from the rain with you on hikes. *Always* be prepared for the worst, because it can happen. Being stuck in the rain on a cool day with no protection could actually kill you."

Sam was thinking about the trash bags Uncle Joe had shown him how to use, when

Pete leaned over and whispered, "Man, she's a laugh a minute. Talk about depressing!"

At that same moment, the tall boy with the goofy grin shouted out, "But maybe it was Old Man Smith that got them!"

There was relieved laughter, and the tall boy waved and wiggled his arms over his head like an attacking ghost and wailed, "Woooooo!" until Shirley had to clap her hands to quiet everyone down.

After Shirley introduced the camp counselors (who were much younger than Shirley and looked like a lot more fun), everyone left for their assigned cabins, dragging backpacks and gear behind them. Sam had been expecting real log cabins, so he was a little disappointed to see that the "cabins" were actually just big cinderblock bunkhouses. Inside, ten or so bunk beds lined the walls, and a big table with chairs around it was placed in the middle of the room. An old yellowed map of the Blue Ridge Mountains was tacked up by the one window at the end of cabin. And a huge, lazy fly buzzed in a monotone in the window.

"Such luxury," Sam said sarcastically as he and Pete threw their stuff on bunks.

"Yeah," Pete agreed. "Luckily, we don't spend much time in here unless it rains. Then we sit around that table and play cards and games until we're bored out of our minds."

"Well, better than being caught out in the rain and dying," Sam said dryly.

Behind him, two boys laughed. One was the tall boy from the shelter meeting. He gave Sam a friendly slap on the back.

"Another funny guy, eh?" he said. "Good. At least there will be someone to take up the slack when I get tired."

The tall boy introduced himself as Jake, and also introduced his friend, Darnell. Like Pete, Jake and Darnell had been to the camp for the past few years, and they had always shared the same cabin.

"Man, I'm just warning you," Darnell said. "Don't take the bunk beneath Jake. They serve a lot, a *lot*, of beans at this camp. And, well, I think you get my point."

"Yeah?" Jake said with a grin. "Well, y'all don't want to sleep above Darnell. His snoring will blast you right out of your bunk and through the ceiling."

This friendly teasing continued as the other 14-year-old boys filed in and claimed bunks, shouting excitedly and unpacking hiking gear. Sam looked around and felt truly happy. It was the first time he'd felt that way in quite a while, and he decided that he was glad he was at Camp Crystal after all. So what if Bart and Alex drove up to the camp? Everyone thought they were jerks. There was nothing to be afraid of.

The rest of the afternoon was spent settling in, taking a tour of the camp, going over the plans for the week, and getting to know the other campers. Shirley told a few more cheery stories about bee stings, poison ivy, and food poisoning. Before dinner in the huge mess hall, everyone had a free hour. Sam and Pete wandered over to the big observation deck that was perched right on the edge of the mountain. It had chairs, a hammock, and even a pair of heavy-duty long-range binoculars mounted on a stand.

"Check it out," Pete said as he focused the binoculars. Sam looked through the lens and, at first, couldn't figure out what he was seeing. Something blue and wavy shimmered, and then a large white bird swooped through the view and landed on the shimmering blue.

"Crystal Lake," Pete explained. "That's where we'll be on Thursday. It's always the best part of the trip. We hike down there, spend the whole day on the lake, and then sleep out on a big grassy lawn under the stars. I mean, unless it's raining. Then everyone has to cram into a huge covered picnic area."

Pete thought about this for a moment and then added, "But that's pretty fun, too."

Sam looked away from the binoculars and down at the lake. It was nestled in the valley between the two mountains, and it was pretty big. Several twisting dirt roads led to it, and Sam could make out a truck traveling along one road.

"So, what is that, like, two miles away?" Sam asked, as he looked through the binoculars again. Now he could see that the truck was pulling a fishing boat. In fact, he could see a number of boats on the lake, some docks, a marina, and a park.

"Things always look closer in the mountains," Pete replied. "Actually, it's about five miles from here. And where the lake ends is an old trail that leads back to what used to be Old Man Smith's land. Everyone always wants to hike there, but then they find out it's about ten miles west of the lake. No one wants to hike *that* far to see a ghost."

A loudly clanging bell made both Pete and Sam jump.

"Dinner!" Pete said. "Wait until that bell wakes you up in the morning. You'll totally jump out of your skin. I don't know why they have to make it so crazy loud."

During dinner, everyone sat in long rows of tables. Just by chance, Deanna ended up sitting directly across from Sam. When she smiled at him again and introduced herself, it made Sam so nervous that he blurted out, "So, you must know a lot about hardware."

Pete snickered, and Sam actually kicked his own leg beneath the table for saying something so stupid.

"Well, I don't exactly hang out a lot around the store, but, yeah, I know a little bit about hammers and nails," Deanna said with a grin.

Somehow, Sam made it through the rest of dinner without saying anything else quite that dumb, but he did get a little tongue-tied and confused whenever Deanna smiled at him. He'd never known a girl with green eyes—at least, not one that kept smiling at him and asking him questions.

"All right everyone. Quiet down!"

Shirley marched to the front of the mess hall as dinner was winding up. Sam quietly pointed out that she had dribbled some ketchup on her starched collar, and this made Deanna and her friend, Kelly, giggle.

"Everyone helps with kitchen cleanup for the next 30 minutes. Then it's 90 minutes around the fire followed by free time until 9:30," Shirley announced briskly. "Then lights out. And when I say lights out, I mean *quiet*!"

"Ah, the first night around the fire," Pete said to Sam, as everyone began clearing dishes. "Watch the 10-year-olds when the Old Man Smith stories get going. If even a twig snaps back in the woods, they all just about fall apart. It's classic."

"Ugh," Deanna said. "I hate those stories. They *still* give me the creeps."

"Well, I'm sure Sam will protect you if you get too scared," Pete said with a grin, as he elbowed Sam and winked at him.

Deanna just smiled shyly and looked away. Sam found himself suddenly hoping that the stories would be the scariest ever.

CHAPTER 6

"**M**ajor yawn," Darnell said in a low voice. He and Jake were sitting on logs right behind Sam and Pete at the very back of the fire ring. "This is only the millionth time I've heard this one."

One of the camp counselors, a young man with a happy smile and dragon tattoos on both forearms, was discussing the "most recent" sightings of the ghost of Old Man Smith.

"Just last week, an old man with a long beard and a cane was seen walking slowly down the road toward Crystal Lake," the counselor said mysteriously. "When a carful of kids stopped to ask him if he wanted a ride, he just turned and stared at them. Then . . ." Here, the counselor paused dramatically and looked around. Some of the youngest kids were hanging on every word.

"Then he raised his cane in the air and shouted. Suddenly, there was a blinding flash of light, a rush of wind and smoke, and then, poof! The old man disappeared into thin air."

"Where did he go?" a breathless voice asked.

Sam looked over and saw that Sara's friend, Vicky, had asked the question. Both Sara and Vicky were wrapped in a blanket and looking fairly worried. The counselor just shrugged.

"That's the thing about ghosts," he said quietly. "Who really understands them? No one. You just never know where they come from or where they're going next. And will they look like ghosts or like us? All we know for sure is that Old Man Smith wanders these hills both day and night."

There was a long moment of dead silence.

Without a sound, Jake picked up a small rock and tossed it over his shoulder into the woods. When it crashed into some dried leaves, an entire row of 10-year-olds jumped about six inches off the long log they were sitting on. Several girls screamed, and Sam was pleased that Deanna briefly grabbed his arm. When everyone turned around to look in the direction of the sound, Jake was looking as ridiculously innocent as he could.

"Darn you, Jake!" Deanna said when she saw his expression.

Everyone laughed, but some of the youngest kids kept glancing nervously at the dark woods anyway. After a few more ghost stories and a stern lecture by Shirley about not putting too much toilet paper in the toilets (lots of stifled giggling), it was time for bed. Sam checked with Sara to make sure she was all right, and then he headed back to his cabin.

At first, Sam thought there was no way he was going to be able to sleep in a room with ten other people—particularly ten 14-year-old boys. Long after the lights were out, there was a lot of chattering, jokes, gross noises, and laughter. At one point, someone flung a dirty sock across the dark room, and it landed right on Sam's face. This created more outbursts of laughter that went on until a tired counselor's booming voice bellowed from a nearby cabin, "Arrow! GO TO SLEEP!"

Somewhere close to midnight the cabin was finally quiet. Sam had never heard such complete silence. Through the open window, the only sounds that drifted in were crickets and a whispering breeze. As it turned out, Darnell didn't snore at all—that had just been another one of Jake's jokes. As Sam grew sleepy, he smiled to himself. It had been a really good day—a day he hadn't expected. He *did* fit in, after all.

Then, just before drifting off, a sound startled Sam awake for a moment. Was it thunder? It was a low rumble; something eerily familiar that Sam couldn't quite put his finger on.

SLAM!

"Oh, man! It's him. . . . He's . . . HE'S OUT THERE! Wake up!"

Sam sat bolt upright in his bunk. He had been asleep barely an hour when someone slammed the cabin door and ran inside, yelling what sounded like a lot of nonsense. Lights flashed on, and there stood Jake in the middle of the room. His hair was wild, and his face was white with terror. He was pointing toward the door and babbling something about ghosts and the bathroom.

"What?" Darnell said, rubbing his eyes. "Slow down, Jake. What are you talking about?"

Jake took a deep breath. Then he tiptoed to the door, barely cracked it open, and peeked out. He stood that way for a full minute while all the boys in the cabin looked at each other and shook their heads.

"I swear he was out there," Jake finally said, as he turned to face the curious stares.

"Who?" Sam asked. "Are you sleepwalking or something?"

Jake shook his head. "No, seriously, I saw an old guy with a cane and a long beard walking between the rows of cabins. When he saw me, he raised his cane in the air and—"

"Old Man Smith!" one of the boys said.

"Oh, come on, Jake," Darnell said, flopping back down on his bunk with a weary sigh. "You woke us all up for a lame joke at 1 a.m.?"

Jake shook his head. "I saw him, Darnell. Really. I was walking to the bathrooms and I heard some footsteps. When I turned around, there was this old guy—beard and torn-up clothes and everything. He lifted his cane, but I didn't wait around to see what was gonna happen next."

The cabin was silent for a moment.

Then, suddenly, high-pitched shrieking came from one of the girls' cabins. In a daze of sleepy and startled confusion, everyone piled out of the cabins to see what was going on.

"There he goes! That's him!" Jake shouted.

All heads turned in the direction Jake was pointing, but all anyone saw was a brief glimpse of a hunched figure disappearing quickly into the dark woods.

"It was that ghost!" Sara came running over to Sam in her jerky steps. Tears were in her eyes. "He . . . he knocked on our window until we woke up. Then when Vicky shined a flashlight at him, he raised up that cane and . . . Oh, Sam, I want to go home!"

Now, all the counselors were milling around in their bathrobes and bare feet. Everyone was talking at once, so nobody heard it.

But Sam did. Off in the distance and headed back down the mountain was the low rumble again. This time, Sam recognized it. It was the roar of Bart's Jeep. Sam was too angry to be scared as he looked at the tears rolling down his sister's cheeks.

"I can absolutely promise you that that was no ghost," Sam said, putting his arm around Sara. "It was just some jerk pulling a prank."

"But he had a beard and an old hat," Sara insisted. "And that cane."

"Yeah," Sam said quietly. "And probably a few beers, too."

"What?" Sara asked, confused.

"Never mind," Sam said. "But you don't need to be scared. It was just a joke. A *really* stupid joke."

It took a while, but the counselors finally calmed everyone down and convinced the campers that it was, in fact, just a prank. This wasn't the first time someone had come up to the camp in the middle of the night, trying to scare everyone. Last year it had been someone running around in a bear costume. The year before that, an entire string of firecrackers had exploded near the youngest girls' cabin at 3 a.m.

"If I ever catch who's doing this . . . " Shirley stood frowning in the middle of all the chaos, with her hands on her hips. Even her bathrobe looked starched, but her short hair was sticking out in about twenty different directions.

For a moment, Sam considered telling Shirley that he knew who it was. But that would be tattling—something only little kids did. And, anyway, he couldn't be absolutely positive it had been Bart and Alex, right? Deep inside, Sam knew that the real reason he didn't want to say anything was that he was afraid—afraid that word would get back to Bart and Alex that he had told on them. And, once again, he hated himself for that. *Still scared*, Sam thought bitterly, as he headed back to his cabin. *I'll never be brave.*

The next day, however, was so beautiful and full of plans that everyone, including Sam, seemed to have forgotten about the night before by the time breakfast was finished. Backpacks were packed, tools were gathered, and everyone grabbed a picnic lunch for the long day of hiking and working. The plan was for the campers to split up into groups of 20 and work along a stretch of trail several miles away from the camp.

"And when they say 'work,' all they really mean is doing a little weeding and digging while having fun," Pete told Sam during breakfast. "There are all sorts of short side trails you can take that lead to lookouts, a fire tower, and a creek with a bunch of beaver dams and gross salamanders."

Sara, who was sitting next to Sam, suddenly looked up from her waffles.

"Beaver dams? Where?" she asked. Sara had read a book once about how beavers had totally changed the direction of a river by building dams. Not only was the story interesting, but also the pictures of the beavers were unbearably cute. She definitely wanted to see one.

Pete just shrugged. "I don't know exactly. Just keep your eyes peeled for the creek. There are a bunch of trails that lead to it."

Groups were chosen, and although Sam was disappointed that Deanna wasn't in his group, he was excited to finally be hiking. The trail went along a ridge on top of the mountain for a couple miles, and Sam could see forever on either side of the mountain. It was like walking along a narrow cloud. Finally, the trail headed down to where Sam's group would be working. Sam stayed near the back to keep an eye on Sara and some of the other younger kids. Since Sam was one of the oldest in the group, the counselor had asked him to be in charge of bringing up the rear.

Until mid-afternoon, everyone worked to clear the trail of rocks and branches and dig small ditches to keep rainwater from flooding the trails. It wasn't really hard work, and now and then the counselor would walk through, handing out candy bars and pointing out unusual birds, rocks, and, once, even a red fox dashing away. Mostly, Sam was looking forward to the hike back, when everyone would meet at the fire tower and take turns climbing it in pairs. He was trying to rev up the courage to ask Deanna to climb with him.

"Hey! There it is!"

Sam looked up, and Sara was pointing down the hillside to a wide creek.

"The beaver creek! And here's a side trail to it like Pete said. Let's go!"

Everyone was taking a rest break for 20 minutes before heading back toward camp and the fire tower. Sam gazed down the hill—the creek really didn't look too far away, and the side trail was pretty well worn down. Obviously, a lot of people had used this trail to go to the creek.

"Okay," Sam said, looking at his watch. "But we can't stay long. We'll just take a quick look and come back."

But Sara was already halfway down the hill and completely ignoring Sam. Sam grinned and followed her. It wasn't often that Sara completely forgot about her limp and just took off. Sam watched her crooked jog and felt happy for his sister. Things had not been easy for her, either. It was good to see her having fun.

Sam finally caught up with Sara when she stopped to inspect a pile of sticks in the creek.

"This is nothing," she said. "Just a bunch of driftwood and weeds. Let's keep going up a little further."

Sam looked back to where they had come from and shook his head.

"We shouldn't go any further than this."

"Come on!" Sara begged. "Just up to that next bend, and then we can turn around. It won't take more than 5 minutes."

"Just to that bend," Sam yelled, as Sara took off again. He definitely didn't want to be gone longer than the break time. It wouldn't look very good on the first day of camp, particularly with him being in charge of the younger campers. Up at the bend, Sara still hadn't found anything, and she kept moving along the creek until Sam's irritated shouts convinced her that she really shouldn't go any further.

The two wandered back toward where the side trail connected to the main trail. Sam kept looking for the muddy strip of trail, but he didn't see it. How could he have missed it? It had seemed so clear when they had walked down it. But now everything began looking the same—just trees and weeds and bushes.

"Shouldn't we be back by now?" Sara asked absently, as she kept looking for dams.

Sam nodded tensely, but didn't speak. He began walking faster. Why couldn't he find it? Had they gone too far? Or not far enough? Now he stopped and doubled back, searching frantically for the trail, running one way and then another.

"Where *is it*?" Sam whispered desperately.

Sara followed behind him, scurrying left and right and giggling at Sam's confusion. Then, suddenly, Sara saw a strange fear in her brother's eyes. She grabbed his arm and pulled him to a stop.

"Sam! Oh no! Are we *lost?*"

CHAPTER 7

"We're not lost!" Sam said angrily.

He wasn't angry at Sara, but he was furious that he had forgotten a very basic rule he'd read a million times in adventure books and in *Real Survival*: he should have left a marker where the side trail ended near the creek. Now he might end up spending 30 minutes or more wandering around down here, looking for that stupid trail. Everyone would be laughing at him when they got back. Getting lost with his little sister, looking for beaver dams!

"Should we yell for help?" Sara asked. Her eyes were wide and startled, and she kept glancing nervously at Sam to see how scared he was.

"No!" Sam barked. The last thing he wanted was for everyone to hear them panicking and yelling. "We're not in any kind of trouble. We just need to find that trail and hurry back. It's not a big deal."

Sam instructed Sara to stay close to him so that they wouldn't get separated. Fifteen minutes later, Sam had followed at least half a dozen worn-down places that looked like trails. But every time they dead-ended in underbrush and thickets. Thirty minutes later, Sam was drenched in sweat, and his hands were shaking. He ran in spurts of sheer terror, then stopped to inspect the ground, and then started running again, yelling at Sara to stay with him. Finally, in a daze, Sam slumped against a tall hickory tree. This *was* a big deal. Things were only getting worse. How far away from the side trail—not to mention the main trail—were they by now?

Then, with a vague sense of relief, Sam realized that surely someone would have noticed they were missing. People were probably looking for them right now.

"Look," Sam said slowly, hoping Sara wouldn't hear his voice shaking. "I think the best thing is to just sit down here for a while and wait until we hear them calling for us. Then we'll call back and forth until we meet up."

Sara stared at her brother. There were some thistles stuck to her shirt, and a small twig was tangled in her hair.

"So we *are* lost," she gasped.

"Well . . . ," Sam began.

"We're going to die!" Sara suddenly cried. "No one will ever find us, and we'll freeze to death like in that story Shirley told!"

"Hey, calm down," Sam said, as he stood up and walked over to his sister. He put his hand on Sara's shoulder. "Our group can't be that far away. I'm sure that when they noticed we were missing, they all started looking for us. They're probably just around the corner and—"

"HELP! WE'RE OVER HERE!" Sara screeched as loudly as she could. "HEEELLLP!"

Sam cringed. He hated the thought of sounding so afraid. Just once, he wanted to be brave and do something right. He didn't want to call for help. He didn't want to be scared. He wanted to be able to calmly lead the two of them out of the woods.

"Why isn't anyone calling back to us?" Sara asked, after she had shouted several times. She turned and looked at Sam. "Why? Where *are* they?"

Then a terrible thought occurred to Sam.

Before the break, the counselor with their group had said that those who wanted to get an early start on the 3-mile hike back to the fire tower could leave right away, instead of taking a break. The counselor and those who stayed behind would bring up the rear. Once everyone reached the tower, they could begin climbing it in pairs.

Now Sam realized what this meant. Everyone would just assume that he and his sister had left early. No one had seen them climb down the side trail. And no one would figure out that they were missing until the rest of the group was miles away! Sam did the math in his head. It was creeping into late afternoon. The sun was quite low and already threatening to drop behind the tallest mountains. There was simply not enough time for the others to discover they were missing and then rescue them before dark.

And there was no way Sam was going to spend a night lost in the wilderness. He wasn't as afraid for himself as he was for Sara, who still occasionally slept with a light on in her room because of nightmares.

"I've got a plan," Sam said hurriedly, as he scanned the mountains surrounding them.

"I think I know how to get us back to Camp Crystal even if we can't find the trail."

"But . . . but what about waiting here?" Sara asked shakily. "I thought you said they'd find us here. Aren't they looking for us?"

"Maybe so," Sam replied carefully. "But if we want to be *sure* to get back before dark, we need to get moving."

The way Sam explained it made sense to Sara. All they had to do was climb back up to the top of the mountain. After all, hadn't they walked along the top of the mountain when they left the camp this morning?

"And when we get to the top, we'll turn right," Sam said, gazing thoughtfully at the hillside. "In about two miles, we should be walking right into the camp just in time for dinner. Easy!"

The two began scrambling up the side of the mountain, but it was far from easy. Loose dirt and rocks made them slip and fall again and again. Thick underbrush full of prickly vines scratched and clawed at their clothing and skin. And the huge trees that they had to constantly walk around made it difficult for Sam to know just how far off course they might be walking. But surely when they reached the top, they would have a better view of exactly where they were.

If only they could get to the top.

"Why aren't we there yet?" Sara finally asked. Dirt and sweat were streaming down her face. "It seems like we've been climbing forever."

Daylight was getting dimmer and dimmer. Sam looked at his watch. It was nearly 6:30. It would be dark in little over an hour, and they hadn't even reached the top of the mountain yet. Things were not looking good. But Sam didn't want to frighten Sara, so he just began moving faster and motioned for her to follow.

"We're nearly there," he called back. "Look! You can see the top."

Through the towering pine, oak, and hickory trees, there did seem to be an opening that looked like a ridge. Sam grabbed at branches to pull himself along faster as the clearing up ahead became brighter.

"Hurry!" he shouted, as Sara began lagging behind. Sam couldn't help but notice that her limp was getting worse as she grew more tired.

Now Sam was practically running, as the steepness of the mountain began leveling out. They had made it! Now all they had to do was follow the ridgeline. Sam turned right and slowed down so Sara could catch up to him.

"I figure we'll be back at the camp in about 30 minutes," Sam said with a weak smile. "But we'll have to walk as fast as we can," he added, looking carefully at Sara, who was now rubbing her knee and frowning. She hated admitting that her leg hurt or slowed her down, but Sam knew.

Now they moved along the ridge, while the sky slowly turned pink and puffy clouds floated lazily on either side of them. Neither Sam nor Sara spoke a word as the woods filled with the sounds of birds and small animals skittering about and preparing for the night. It briefly occurred to Sam that all of this would have been pretty awesome if he weren't worried half out of his mind. When a cool evening breeze picked up, Sam began moving faster and encouraged Sara with occasional shouts of "Almost there!"

Then, all of a sudden, the soft grass along the ridge disappeared. Loose rocks and sand replaced it. There were no longer any trees. In a flash, Sam noticed that the air around him had stopped smelling woodsy and warm. Instead, a cold wind whipped his face. Then the ridge instantly gave way to a wide-open nothingness.

"Whoa! Oh no!" Sam shouted and fell backward in a skid. Barely five yards in front of him, the ridge abruptly ended, and a sheer cliff wall dropped for nearly 1,000 feet. Pebbles from Sam's skid toppled over the ledge and fell forever, soundlessly in the cold wind. Behind Sam, Sara stopped quickly and gasped at the sight.

"What's this?" Sara sputtered. "Where's the camp? I thought you said . . . Where *are* we?"

"Well . . . ," Sam said breathlessly as he sat up and tried to calm down. "I'm not exactly sure."

Sara stood staring at her brother with her mouth open. Then she angrily kicked at a rock. "You *don't know?*" she nearly screamed. "You told me it was only 30 minutes away, and now you don't even know where we are? Vicky told me that Alex said you were a loser. No wonder he stopped hanging out with you!"

Sam looked at Sara for a moment. It wasn't often that she lost her temper or fought with him. Sam struggled briefly with his anger at Alex. Then he looked out at the wide open space. For the first time in days, the last thing on his mind had been Alex and Bart. That all seemed so distant—so unimportant. It seemed particularly unimportant at this very moment. Sam took a deep breath and turned back around to Sara. Sitting beneath a tall pine tree, she was looking a little teary and regretful at her outburst.

"Look," Sam said, trying to sound as confident as possible. "We're going to get out of this, Sara. I promise. Maybe we should have turned left instead of right, but we can't be too far from camp. Just let me figure this out."

Sara just nodded and wiped her nose on her sleeve. For a long time, Sam stood very still with his arms folded, thinking hard while his heart pounded painfully. *We're lost*, he finally admitted to himself and felt a little sick. *Completely and totally lost.* How many books and stories had he read about getting lost in the wilderness? Every single time, the very first and most important rule was always the same: stay where you are. Don't try to find your way back—wait for help to come to you. And now Sam had done just the opposite. He had fallen right into the panic trap. Who knows how far off course he had led them?

In anger and frustration, Sam threw a handful of rocks over the ledge and shouted, "It's not fair!"

This behavior frightened Sara, who began to ask a stream of startled questions while Sam tried to calm her down. Then, in a flood of thoughts, he ran through the events of the past few days to see if anything, even some small detail, might help them. But the only thing that kept replaying in his mind was Shirley standing in the picnic shelter, wagging her finger and saying, "Always be prepared for the worst, because it can happen."

And now it had. The last of the daylight was rapidly slipping away.

Sam and Sara were going to have to spend the night on the mountain.

CHAPTER 8

"Quick," Sam said. "You need to gather as many long branches as you can find." He had suddenly snapped out of his fog of fear and worry. As the very serious danger of their situation became real, Sam's mind cleared.

Distant thunder was beginning to rumble closer as the purple sunset dipped behind rainclouds. There was no time to waste. Without asking why, Sara began limping around and picking up the longest branches she could carry. Meanwhile, Sam moved back down the mountainside until he reached a point where the wind was blocked. Then he began searching for a fallen tree.

It was the most basic of shelters, but it was one Sam had studied with curiosity when he read about a young woman who had gotten lost in the Rockies. The woman had simply found a fallen tree that leaned at an angle from its stump. Then she cleared out a space beneath the tree and leaned branches on either side of the trunk like a tent. She stuffed leaves and twigs in the spaces between the branches all the way to where the trunk met the ground. This left only a small opening near the stump for her to crawl in and out of.

Seven nights, Sam thought to himself as he looked for the perfect fallen tree. The woman had slept in this shelter for seven nights in very cold temperatures. Falling snow had piled on top of the shelter, actually adding to the insulation. When the woman was finally rescued, she was very hungry and exhausted—but she had survived. That was all that mattered, Sam thought. *Survival.*

"Over here!" Sam called to Sara. He had found a moderately big tree that had fallen not long ago. Many of its branches still had drying leaves on it, which would help add to the protection it would give. Sara hobbled over and dropped a stack of sticks and branches near the stump of the tree.

"First, we need to clear out a space under here," Sam said, pointing to the ground beneath the trunk. "Then we'll start building the walls with the branches by leaning them like this."

Sara just nodded blankly when Sam showed her how the shelter would be constructed. Her eyes were huge and unblinking. *She's in shock*, Sam worried. He never said the word "shelter" or mentioned anything about spending the night alone on the mountain. It was now just a bitter fact that Sam had to face as bravely as possible while comforting Sara in any way he could. They worked in silence for a long while, clearing a floor space all the way down to the dirt. Then they lined the branches close together, and stuffed the gaps with leaves and twigs.

Closer now, the low thunder grumbled, and the first heavy drops of rain splattered on the trees. Darkness had just begun to settle in.

"Hurry," Sam said quietly, as he opened his backpack and pulled out a flashlight and the box of big, black, heavy-duty trash bags. He handed two to Sara.

"Make holes for your head and arms," he instructed. "Wear it like a raincoat. Fill the other one up with pine needles and leaves as fast as you can."

In spite of Shirley's dismal warnings about the dangers of rain, neither Sam nor Sara had brought a raincoat that day. It had been warm and cloudless in the morning, and the hike would be long over before dark. Sam had figured that the box of trash bags would be more than enough.

As a clap of thunder boomed across the sky, Sam made his own "raincoat." Then he filled another bag with pine needles and threw it inside the shelter. Next he hurriedly covered the shelter with a layer of trash bags, tucking the edges around branches to make it as watertight as possible. Just as Sam and Sara were scurrying into their shelter, the clouds, as if on cue, opened up and began to pour. Sam hung one more trash bag over the small opening near the trunk of the tree.

Once inside, Sam and Sara huddled on their stuffed bags and just stared at one another for a few minutes as they tried to catch their breath. It was damp and smelled strongly of dirt inside the shelter, and there was barely enough room for Sam and Sara to stretch out their legs. But it was remarkably rainproof. As Sam listened to the rain clatter on the trash bags, he felt a glimmer of pride in spite of his fear. At least he'd done one thing right.

Finally, Sam pulled his backpack in front of

him and handed Sara the flashlight to shine on it.

"Take inventory," he said. "That's the third rule."

"The third rule of what?" Sara asked in a shaky voice. At least she was speaking now.

"The third rule of what you do when you get lost in the wilderness," Sam said, as he began pulling everything out of his backpack. "The first rule is 'Don't panic.'" He paused and looked at his sister. "So, yeah, I pretty much blew that one."

Sara just shrugged and steadied the flashlight.

"The second rule is 'Find shelter.' Done. And now we have to take inventory of everything we have. Even the smallest things might be important."

Sam had carried everything he and Sara needed on the hike so that she wouldn't have to carry a pack. Now he was both grateful and disappointed that he had grabbed his pack when he followed Sara down the side trail to the creek. He was glad to have the handful of things that could keep them alive until they were rescued. But he couldn't help but wonder whether they'd already be rescued if he had left the pack behind. Someone might have seen it. It would have set off the alarm that something wasn't right.

But there was little point in thinking about that now.

"Okay. Four bottles of water, four candy bars, a pack of gum, and a bag of animal crackers," Sam said, placing the food in a pile. "That's our store of food until . . . well, until they find us."

Sara looked at the small pile. She'd been too scared to even think about being hungry, but now the candy bars were looking pretty good. She hadn't had anything to eat since lunch nearly seven hours earlier. She reached for one, but Sam pulled it away quickly.

"Not tonight," he said. "We have to wait until morning. You know, to space it out. We can split a bottle of water, but that's it."

"But they'll find us tomorrow, won't they?" Sara asked in a small voice. In the dim glow of the flashlight, she looked exhausted and pale with worry.

"I hope so," was all Sam said, taking a long drink.

Two tee shirts, a pocket knife that Uncle Joe had given Sam at the last minute, a stapled-together itinerary and list of rules for Camp Crystal, another flashlight (the counselor had said they might explore a cave if they had time), and a small bag containing a tiny mirror with a pink handle, three big pink hair ties in it, and a small bottle of *Handy Dandy* hand sanitizer. These were the entire contents of Sam's backpack.

Sam stared at everything and then picked up the hair ties and *Handy Dandy*.

"Well, thank goodness we have these," Sam said with a straight face. "I mean, in case we have a hairdo emergency or get some dirt on our hands."

For just a moment, Sara smiled and even managed a small giggle. Then her face grew serious again.

"Sam, what are we going to do?" she asked. "Are we going to try finding the camp tomorrow or just stay here?"

Sam thought for a while and fiddled with the pocketknife. "I don't know yet. Maybe we can get an idea of where we are in the daylight. We'll see."

For a long time, Sara and Sam just sat huddled together, listening to the rain. Little puddles had gathered on the shelter, and now there was a steady dripping around them. Even so, they had managed to stay fairly dry. The cold wind was blocked by the mountain and the shelter, so Sam wasn't worried about hypothermia. In fact, it was almost a little stuffy inside the trash bags.

"Twenty-four hours ago, if anyone had told me I'd be sitting around in the dark underneath a dead tree wearing a trash bag, I totally would not have believed them," Sam finally said, making his sister giggle a bit again.

"Can we leave the flashlight on all night?" Sara asked hopefully.

"No way," Sam said. "We have to save the batteries as much as we can. We should probably turn it off now and try to sleep."

"But it's so dark and . . . ," Sara began in a panicked voice.

Sam put his hand on her back. "Don't worry. I'm right here. You can hold onto the other flashlight, but don't turn it on unless you absolutely have to."

Once the flashlight was off, it was pitch black. Sam held his hand three inches from his face and couldn't even see it. Outside, the storm and the rain were moving away, which was good. But now, without the pattering of rain on the shelter roof, the sounds of the night woods seemed louder: hooting, rustling, and creaking. Next to him, Sam could feel Sara shaking. He wasn't sure if she was crying or shivering from fear—or both.

"Remember that time when Mom took us to that beach along Chesapeake Bay?" Sam began. "And we watched that guy catching crabs?"

Sometimes when Don scared or hurt Sara, Sam brought up better times and memories to calm down his sister and make her sleepy. It almost always worked. So now, lost in the middle of the Blue Ridge Mountains at night, Sam found himself recalling a summer weekend from three years ago. He rambled on about crabs and cotton candy and waves until Sara stopped shaking. Sometime later, he could tell by her breathing that she had fallen asleep.

Sam closed his eyes and listened to the very distant thunder rolling away to the east. He shifted the bag of pine needles until he was as close to comfortable as he was going to get. At last, in spite of everything, he began drifting off. Fitful dream images of walking through the forest kept running through his head, but finally Sam fell asleep.

Much later, in the dead of the night, Sam was dreaming of a neighbor's dog, Bruiser, digging for a bone. Digging . . . digging . . .

Suddenly Sam's eyes flew open.

"Wh-what?" Sam gasped, and sat bolt upright, his heart pounding painfully. Next to him, Sara was still asleep. But Sam gripped his flashlight and listened with dread.

It was no dream. Something was moving around and digging just outside the shelter.

CHAPTER 9

Sam held his breath and waited. Whatever was outside kept digging and rooting around and then stopping for a few minutes. It seemed to be waiting to see what Sam would do. There was a definite sharp smell like wet fur, and every now and then the animal grunted and snuffed. And there was a heaviness to its footfalls—this was definitely not just some curious raccoon or sleepless squirrel.

"Sam?" Sara suddenly sat up in the dark.

"Shhh," Sam said as quietly as possible. "Don't turn on your flashlight yet. Something's outside."

"*What?*" Sara whispered loudly, and immediately began fumbling for her flashlight. "I'm not sitting here in the pitch black and—"

"Wait! I think . . . I think it might be a bear, and I don't want to startle it," Sam said nervously. His mouth had gone dry and his legs were numb from sitting so still. "Maybe it will just go away if we're quiet."

Sam felt Sara jump and gasp when he said the word "bear."

"Don't be scared," he whispered. "It's not interested in us."

It was true that the bear, if that's what it was, was definitely not interested in Sam and Sara. Sam knew that bears rarely attack people unless the bear's cubs are nearby. But (and this is what was making Sam's heart race even faster) there was something a bear might want *from* Sam and Sara. Tucked in the bottom of the backpack, beneath two shirts and three bottles of water, were the gum, candy bars, and animal crackers. It didn't matter that they were all wrapped and hidden away. The bear could smell them.

Two thousand times better than a human's sense of smell, Sam thought desperately, as he strained to hear what the animal outside was doing. He remembered hearing about a bear that had smelled a rotting watermelon from seven miles away and torn apart a metal garbage can to get to it. What might this bear do to a stick-and-trash-bag shelter to get to a Snickers bar?

Whoof, whoof! Now the snuffing sounded like it was only inches from the shelter. The animal smell became stronger, and heavy pawing and scratching shook some of the thin limbs leaning on the dead tree trunk. Sara grabbed Sam's arm and let out a little shriek. Outside, the animal was suddenly quiet again. Then it sounded as though it were moving slowly back into the woods. Sam sighed. Maybe it was leaving. Maybe it hadn't even been a bear. Maybe—

WHOOF!!

All at once, the thumping of four legs grew louder. The bear was back! Now it took a swipe at the shelter with one of its long-clawed paws. Leaves and limbs and dripping trash bags caved in on Sam and Sara, as Sara cowered and screamed something that Sam couldn't make out.

"No! Back! No!" Sam shouted at the bear he still couldn't see. He hadn't wanted to startle the bear. But now that it was clear that the bear knew he and Sara were in the shelter, Sam hoped the loud noises would scare it away. He knew that the kind of bears that lived in the Blue Ridge Mountains weren't usually aggressive. In fact, they preferred to be as far away from loud humans as possible.

"GO AWAY!" Sam bellowed, as he clapped his shaking hands and then banged his flashlight against the tree trunk.

Complete silence.

But Sam could still smell the bear. And he could hear it breathing. This bear was determined to find the snacks hidden in the bottom of Sam's backpack. Somehow, Sam had to move the backpack away from the shelter. But even if the bear got what it wanted, wouldn't it keep hanging around for more? Still, Sam had to do *something*. He and Sara couldn't just sit in the shelter, worrying and waiting.

"It doesn't want us—just the food," Sam said shakily to Sara, who was now crying and huddled on the ground with the bag of pine needles over her head. Slowly, Sam pulled out the candy and gum and cookies. "I'm going to throw the food out to it, and hopefully—"

But Sam never got to finish the sentence. In a mighty clattering of limbs, the bear wiped out one entire side of the shelter. Both Sam and Sara screamed and fell backward. There was a terrific confusion of leaves and loud noises and panic as Sam struggled to point his flashlight at the bear, which was now panting and making some terrible growling sounds. The beam of light settled for just a moment on a wall of moving black fur, and that was all Sam needed to see.

"Run!" Sam shouted at Sara. He grabbed her under her arm, lifted her up, and pushed her away from the bear with a mighty shove.

In a terrible slow-motion blur, Sam heard Sara scurrying off in one direction while the bear closed in on him from the other. Or rather, the bear was closing in on the scent of the food still clutched in Sam's hand. A quick jolt of flashlight lit up a long snout and dark, shining eyes. The foul animal smell seemed to overwhelm Sam, as the bear lunged toward him. All at once, Sam hurled the food to the ground and turned to leap away from the crushed shelter, but a heavy thud and a searing pain in his arm sent him reeling backward. Almost as an afterthought, the bear had swatted at Sam as it lumbered toward the food. The weight of the swat knocked the wind out of Sam, and three long claw marks down his left arm were already streaming blood.

"Sam!" Sara cried out from some distance away.

"Keep moving!" Sam managed to croak. "I . . . I'm all right."

There was a crackling of wrappers as the bear zeroed in on the food. Sam staggered away as quickly as he could while gasping for air. He looked back only once to make sure the bear wasn't following him. In the dim light, he could see the bear sitting back on its haunches calmly eating one of the candy bars. If Sam hadn't been so terrified, he might have laughed at the sight. As it was, he moved as quickly as he could through the dark woods toward Sara.

"Your arm!" Sara gasped when Sam reached her. "Did it bite you?"

Sam took only a moment to look at the claw marks. They were long, but not terribly deep. Even so, his entire arm was now dripping with blood that splattered the trash bag he was still wearing.

"No, just a scratch," Sam said quietly. "But we need to get away from here before I can take care of it."

Sam led the way, having no idea where they were going except away from the bear. They stumbled through the forest for nearly twenty minutes before Sam felt it was safe to stop. He and Sara leaned against a huge tree, catching their breath. Sam's arm felt like it was on fire, and he could feel his pulse pounding in the pain of the scratches. Some of the bleeding had stopped, but his arm was a mess of dried blood, dirt, and sweat. As much as he hated doing it, he was going to have to use one of the bottles of water to clean it.

"Does it hurt?" Sara asked, when she got a closer look at the long scratches Sam was wiping down with one of the tee shirts.

"Not really," Sam lied. "Just a little sting."

"Weren't you scared?"

Sam just nodded. "Of course. A freaking bear took a swing at me."

"But you made sure I was safe first," Sara said, with both wonder and admiration.

Sam just nodded again as he went to work on the third scratch, wincing at the pain. When he was done, he turned the tee shirt inside out and wrapped it around his arm. High above the trees, the sky was beginning to turn a bluish gray with just a hint of pink. Off in the distance, several blue jays loudly announced the arrival of morning. The long night alone in the mountains was nearly over.

"You know," Sara said quietly after a long while, "I don't *really* think you're a loser."

Now Sam and Sara were down to two bottles of water and no food at all. The dull ache of last night's hunger had become a gnawing pain, and as the two of them sat waiting for the sun to spill over the mountainside, their stomachs made a constant racket of growling and grumbling. Sam thought briefly about the breakfast he'd had just yesterday morning— piles of pancakes, seven sausages, a banana, orange juice, and even a chocolate cupcake (someone put those out by mistake). But it was just torture thinking of that. No sense making things worse.

"A cheeseburger," Sara suddenly said, as though reading her brother's mind. "A huge cheeseburger and two orders of fries—no, three. That's what I'm having after they find us today."

She looked at Sam out of the corner of her eye.

"Because they will find us today, right?"

Sam nodded. "I can't imagine how they couldn't. I mean, we can't be *that* far away from the camp."

"I just can't think of spending another night with . . . ," Sara shuddered, "with all this stuff out here."

At that very moment, just as the sun crept over the mountain, they heard a strange clang.

It seemed to be coming from higher up on the mountain, and it sounded like someone banging a hammer on metal over and over again.

"What's that?" Sara asked. "Is it . . . are they trying to get us to yell back?"

Sam listened. The sound seemed vaguely familiar. Sam suddenly snapped his fingers.

"The dinner bell!" he nearly shouted. "It's the camp's dinner bell ringing for breakfast."

Sam looked at his watch. It was 6:30—the exact time the morning bell rang.

"And it's coming from right up there," Sara said excitedly, pointing to a ridge to their left. But even as she said this, the noise seemed to shift and come from across the mountain and to their right.

"Or over there?" Sara asked doubtfully.

Then the clanging drifted across the valley, sounding as if it had come from an entirely different mountain—and then from yet another mountain even farther away. Then it faded to a distant hum and stopped altogether.

"Echoes," Sam sighed and slumped against the tree. "The bell is echoing off every mountain. It's impossible to tell where it came from."

"But at least we heard it," Sara said hopefully. "That means we're close, right? That means it'll be easy to find us, huh?"

Sam nodded, but he knew that loud sounds like the dinner bell could travel for miles in the mountains. And even though he didn't want to think about it, he couldn't help recalling Shirley's story about the two teens who had gotten lost and died. Their bodies were found only a few miles away from the trail. With a sinking feeling of dread, it occurred to Sam that he and Sara were in serious danger, no matter how close or far away they might be from Camp Crystal.

"We should just stay where we are," Sam said. "It seems like the best idea. It's what I should have had us do yesterday."

But two, and then three, and finally four hours later, Sam began second-guessing his decision. Where *were* the rescuers? Maybe he and Sara should climb back up to the ridge to get a better view. However, after running from the bear in the middle of the night, Sam really had no idea where the ridge was anymore. But was just sitting and doing nothing really the best idea? Sam made a mental list of bad things:

Both he and Sara were growing weak with hunger.

There were now only two bottles of water left, and being without water would be far worse than being without food.

Sara's limp was the worst he'd ever seen it.

His arm felt like it was on fire, and it was swelling badly.

And nightfall was eight hours away.

Nightfall, Sam thought. He didn't know if he could stand the horror of another night out here. And he couldn't help but notice that the air was noticeably cooler today. Chilly, even. What if it dipped below freezing tonight? What if . . .

Sara heard it first.

"Sam! Listen! Here they come!"

Out over the valley was a heavy whirring noise, and it was getting closer. It was the sound of a helicopter.

CHAPTER 10

"Down here! Here we are!"

Sam and Sara peered through the trees and could see the helicopter hovering first in one spot and then in another as it searched for them. They waved their arms frantically and jumped up and down and shouted. But it was no good. They were too hidden by the thick late-summer forest. At one point, the helicopter was practically directly overhead, and Sam ran as hard as he could to get to an open patch of grass on the ridge. But all he managed to do was trip over roots and fall on his arm, starting the bleeding all over again.

"Wait! WE'RE HERE!!" Sam screamed up at the treetops. "Look down!! Down HERE!" The helicopter hovered for several seconds and then took off again. Now the sound of its blades was getting more and more distant.

It disappeared across the valley as it moved to another hillside and hovered there.

"No!" Sara yelled in desperation. "Come back!"

She'd been limping behind Sam, and now she sat down on the ground and began crying and hitting the dirt with her fists. Sam came over and kneeled next to her in silence. His face was white with fear. He was so stunned by what had just happened that he didn't even notice the blood streaming from his arm down onto his jeans and shoes.

"This isn't good," he choked out. He'd been trying to stay brave for the sake of Sara, but this was just too much. "They . . . they think we're not here."

Sara put her face in her hands. Far off in the distance, the noise of the helicopter disappeared completely. All that was left was the whistling of a chilly breeze and the racket of irritated crows in a nearby tree.

"But they have to come back and check again when they don't find us," Sara said suddenly, as muddy streaks of tears dripped down her cheeks. "Don't they? They have to be sure, right? They can't just check once and never come back!"

Sam stared at his sister. She was right! Surely they'd fly back over again later this afternoon—maybe even sooner. There was no time to waste. It hadn't occurred to Sam that a helicopter would be used in the search, and now he really wished he'd thought of that sooner. He knew all about distress signals. Sam had read about sending flares into the sky from out at sea and even setting a car's tires on fire in the desert. There were a million ways to catch the attention of rescuers flying overhead.

Sam grabbed Sara and hugged her. "That's right! Wow, good thinking. Come on. We need to hurry. Let me show you what to do."

Sam and Sara struggled up to the flat, open space on the ridge. With any luck, the returning searchers would see them without the help of a distress signal, but Sam didn't want to take any chances.

"It's pretty simple," Sam explained to Sara. "All we need to do is make three big piles of limbs, rocks, or whatever, right next to each other. We have to make them big enough so that there's no way anyone in that helicopter can miss them."

"Why three?" Sara asked, as she began gathering sticks.

"It's what's known as the 'mountain distress signal,'" Sam explained. "Anything on a mountain in a group of three means someone's in real trouble."

"Well, that's totally us," Sara said, as she began a pile. But Sara was moving very slowly now. And after every few armfuls of sticks, she had to sit down for a while. Sam opened the next-to-last bottle of water and split it with her. Since the weather was cool and they had been sitting in one place, neither Sam nor Sara had sweated much today, but Sam knew they were still very dehydrated. And that was dangerous. Sam wouldn't allow himself to think about it too much, but if he and Sara were not rescued very soon, they could be in serious trouble. One final bottle of water between two people would not last long.

Because of his swollen and painful arm, Sam could use only one hand for picking up rocks and limbs. He had formed a kind of sling with the bloodied tee shirt, but even the slightest movement sent burning jolts of pain through his arm all the way up to his shoulder. It was very slow going, but finally, Sam and Sara managed to make three fairly large piles right next to each other. They had placed them in a wide, grassy area, so there was no way searchers in a helicopter could possibly miss them when they came back around again.

"Listen," Sam said quietly, as he tilted his head. "Can you hear it?"

Sam and Sara had been sitting next to the piles for nearly an hour when a distant rumble seemed to promise the arrival of the helicopter and their rescue.

"Yes!" Sara said excitedly, as she scanned the sky. Then her excitement faded and her face fell as she pointed behind them. Coming up over a far mountain were some of the darkest clouds Sam had ever seen. These were not dull gray rainclouds, like those that had moved in yesterday evening. This was a fast-moving storm that looked pretty violent even from miles away. Jagged lightning flashed and crackled. What Sam thought was a helicopter was actually the crashing of distant thunder. This was a thunderstorm.

A terrible image raced through Sam's mind.

Several years earlier, a group of four hikers were moving across a mountaintop in the Smoky Mountains just as a lightning-packed storm approached rapidly. The group paused for just a while to watch the terrifying storm move in. But the storm was moving faster than they had anticipated. All at once, there was a massive roll of thunder, and the storm was upon them.

They scurried over to a rock ledge and huddled beneath it to get out of the pelting rain. But a rocky mountaintop is like a lightning rod. Strike after strike of lightning hit the rocks around the hikers, and they could hear a charged buzz with every bolt. It was as if the storm had electrified the rocks around the hikers, and now they were trapped inside. Suddenly, there was a tremendous bang, a flash of blue light, and the smell of burned hair and flesh. A lightning strike had hit just outside the ledge and then traveled through one of the metal hiking sticks and into the body of one of the hikers. It killed her instantly, burning her up like a piece of paper.

"We have to get moving back down the mountain!" Sam said as he jumped to his feet. "We can't be out in this open area in a storm."

Sara looked devastated. She waved her arm toward the three piles. "But . . . we have to wait for them to see this. The helicopter . . . "

"There won't be any more helicopters for a while with that coming in," Sam said bitterly, as he pointed to the storm. It was racing toward them at an alarming pace. "Hurry!"

But there was no more hurrying for Sara. Exhausted, terrified, hungry, and dehydrated, she dragged behind Sam, limping heavily. At first, Sam was irritated and kept shouting for his sister to keep up with him. The wind was picking up, and the tall oak trees were swaying and groaning above them. They had to get further down the mountain and find some kind of shelter before the storm hit. Otherwise, at best, they would get soaking wet. At worst, they would run the risk of being fried to a crisp by lightning.

Finally, Sam grabbed a sturdy stick he found on the ground. He whipped out the jackknife and quickly trimmed away the stray branches on it. It wasn't exactly a masterpiece, but it would do.

"Here," he said, handing the walking stick to Sara. "This should make things a little easier."

The stick made all the difference. They managed to move far enough away from the open ridge to be safe from lightning strikes. But what to do about shelter? There wasn't enough time to build another shelter from a fallen tree. Nor were there enough trash bags left to provide waterproofing. Both Sam and Sara had worn their bags all day for a little extra warmth, and now the bags were shredded and muddy. Quickly, Sam pulled out two new bags, and he and Sara fashioned second "raincoats" to wear over their tattered ones. This would at least provide a little protection from what promised to be a terrific downpour.

"That's a cold wind," Sara mumbled hollowly, as she poked her arms through the bag. Then she sadly whispered, "Hypothermia."

Sam looked carefully at Sara. Her face drooped, and her shoulders slumped. She was showing the first signs of giving up. Sam grabbed both her shoulders and gave her a little shake.

"We're not going to die," he said firmly. "You *know* they're looking for us. Somebody will see our signal. It's going to turn out all right. I promise."

But Sam had serious doubts about whether he could keep that promise. A bad storm would keep helicopters and searchers away for the rest of the afternoon. It would also very possibly destroy the three piles of branches and stones they had made. He and Sara would be back to square one—and back to another night alone in the mountains. But he couldn't dwell on that now. The flashes of lightning and the booms of thunder were only seconds apart now. The storm was bearing down on them, and bringing cold air with it.

Sam's eyes swept back and forth, desperately looking for anything to take cover under. Even a grove of thick bushes or a stand of low trees or . . .

There! Just a bit further down the hill was an outcropping of stone and huge rocks. And right in the center of the rocks was a big, dark hole.

"A cave!" Sam shouted and grabbed Sara's hand to pull her along. "Perfect!"

"Perfect?" Sara said doubtfully, as she stumbled beside Sam. The cave looked pretty uninviting. The rocks glistened with a slimy dampness, and just beyond the entrance, it was absolutely pitch black. Furry green moss lined the rocks leading into the cave. "Are you sure it's safe?" Sara asked. "Don't bears—"

"Not this time of year," Sam said quickly. "And it'll be a lot safer than being out in this storm."

Sam dug out the two flashlights, and he and Sara crouched down and crawled through the cave entrance. Once inside, there was room to stand up. It was strangely quiet. The wind, noises of the woods, and hum of insects were suddenly muffled and far away. It was like being inside of a rock. Sam and Sara shined their flashlights toward the back of the cave and could see that it went on for nearly thirty yards or more. It was hard to tell if it turned and continued past the beam of their lights.

"Wow," Sam said quietly. "It's a real cave, not just some hole in the rocks."

Outside, the rain was suddenly driving down sideways in a howling wind. But inside the cave, it was completely dry. And the floor of the cave was covered in soft, piled sand. Sam couldn't believe their good luck. He and Sara ventured further back into the cave.

"Ugh," Sara said, as she fanned the air in front of her. "What is that *smell*? It's totally gross."

Sam had figured the inside of a cave would smell musty, but this was something different, something sharper and rotting. But more disturbing than the terrible odor was what was happening near the back of the cave. It had started as a ticking, then a rustling, and then the whole cave seemed to vibrate. Was it just the sound of the rain hitting the rocks outside?

Sam carefully directed the beam of his flashlight all around the floor of the cave. Nothing. Up the walls, the light slowly crept. Still nothing. Then, at the same time, both he and Sara shined light on the ceiling of the cave.

And there it was.

Sara reeled backwards and gasped. Thousands of bats were hanging from the rocky ceiling, fluttering their leathery wings!

CHAPTER 11

"Eeeek!" Sara shrieked and headed toward the entrance of the cave in a hurry with her hands over her head. Sam was close behind her. But outside, the rain was coming down in sheets, and the wind was so strong that some of the smaller trees were bent in half. Sam and Sara were trapped between a huge bat colony and a terrible storm. The two huddled just inside the entrance of the cave, breathing in the fresh air.

"Bat poop," Sam said with a grimace. "That's what stinks. Probably a foot deep back there where they're all hanging. Just be glad we saw them before we walked into *that*."

Sara glanced nervously into the dark behind them. The rustling of bat wings stopped once she and Sam moved away from the back of the cave.

"We're not going to stay in here with all those bats, are we?"

A mighty crash of thunder shook the rock walls of the cave, and a gust of bitter air whooshed by. Sam waited for the echoes of the thunder to die down.

"Well, we sure can't go out into that," Sam replied. He looked at his watch. It was already late afternoon, and the storm showed no signs of letting up. There was very little chance that anyone was out searching for them in this weather and absolutely no chance that the helicopter was coming back. The best they could do was stay put. Sam glanced over at Sara. She was so exhausted that she had practically fallen asleep between her question and Sam's answer. Her head hung down and to the side as she sat leaning against the cave wall.

Sam noticed that part of the rock wall tucked in and away from the entrance. It was something like a small room within the cave. Enough light from the cave opening streamed in to keep the side cave room fairly well lit. And inside of it, the air was not nearly as cold. Sam placed his hand on the curved rock wall and could feel that the rocks were still warm from what had been, until the storm, a sunny day.

Sam spread two trash bags on the soft sand floor and pulled out the other tee shirt and wadded it up to use as a pillow. Then he woke Sara up and led her in.

"But if we sleep in here, how will they find us before nighttime?" Sara asked, her eyes barely open.

"It's okay," Sam murmured, as Sara stretched out. "Just try to sleep. It's safe in here."

But Sara was already lightly snoring.

Sam drank the last of the final bottle of water. Then he pulled out his jackknife and quietly cut the tops off the four empty water bottles (he'd saved every one) to make them more like cups. After this, he placed the four cups just outside the cave in the pouring rain. In no time at all, the cups were full. Sam greedily drank all four and put them back in the rain. When they were full again, he brought them in and placed them near Sara so she could drink when she woke up.

Three minutes without air, three days without water, and three weeks without food. Sam mentally reviewed the "rule of threes" he had often read about in *Real Survival.* A human could live only so long without air, water, or food. Luckily, there was no lack of air, and along with the creeks and the rain, he and Sara would probably have enough water. But food? It hadn't even been two full days, but Sam felt as if he could happily eat the leaves on the trees.

Sam leaned against the warm stone wall and closed his eyes, remembering the dinner Uncle Joe had cooked the night before he and Sara left for Camp Crystal. There had been thick grilled steaks, mashed potatoes with mushroom gravy, and the kind of green beans with fried onions that Sam usually had only at Thanksgiving. Uncle Joe had also made soft rolls with honey butter, and dessert was strawberry shortcake with huge, fresh strawberries and whipped cream.

Sam drifted into a half-asleep daze of food memories. Then he fell into dreams of huge sandwiches that were just out of reach, and five-layer cakes that floated away into the sky.

Sometime later, silence woke him up. The rain had stopped, and a slice of red sunlight filled the cave entrance. Sara was still asleep, but Sam noticed that two of her cups of water were gone, so she must have woken up at some point. Quietly, Sam picked up the empty cups and tiptoed to the entrance. He could hear water streaming off the rocks. He knew that it might not be the cleanest water, dripping off a bat-filled cave. But it was better than nothing.

As the cups filled, Sam watched evening come to the mountains. The sunset was amazing, and all of the trees glistened with rain. Birds whistled back and forth, even though a cold wind had cleared the air. Huge pink clouds rolled lazily across the sky. In spite of everything, Sam was awed by the beauty of it all.

Nature is neither cruel nor kind. It is indifferent. Sam thought about this quote he had read in one of his magazines not long ago. At the time, he wasn't sure what it meant, but now he thought he understood. Nature and these woods around him were not bullies, like Alex and Bart. They didn't mean to hurt or frighten him—not the bear, the storms, the darkness, or the bats. Nor did nature care about Sam. He and Sara were truly on their own in this strange, wonderful, and sometimes terrible new world. Somehow these thoughts made Sam feel better and braver. The wilderness was not an enemy.

At this very moment, Sam heard a humming from far back in the cave. Then there was a whirring and the flapping of thousands of tiny wings. All at once, every bat streamed out of the cave in what looked like a long, thin, black cloud. Sam barely had time to duck. The wings of several bats even brushed the top of his head as they flew out into the evening. Then every one of them disappeared into specks in the purple sky.

Sam was startled, but not afraid.

Not afraid, he thought, as he walked back into the cave with the cups of water for Sara. Thankfully, Sara had slept through the exit of the bats.

And tomorrow we'll be rescued. I'll make sure of that.

With this new confidence, Sam lay down on the still-warm sand and closed his eyes. Deep, dreamless sleep came to him immediately. It wasn't until many hours later that a rustling hum awakened him. It was the bats returning just before sunrise.

"What was that?" Sara asked groggily in the darkness, reaching for her flashlight.

"Just the wind," Sam said quietly.

Sara drifted back to sleep, but now Sam was wide awake. Something was wrong. He could feel his heart beating in his bear-scratched arm—a constant burning, throbbing sensation. When he tried to move his arm, it barely budged. Quietly, Sam unwound the old tee shirt that was now covered with dirt and dried blood. When he shined his flashlight on the scratches, he nearly got sick. All three were a sickly, unnatural shade of red and full of pus that was oozing out in little streams. His arm had swollen to almost twice its normal size, and a bad smell drifted up to his nose.

Infection—really bad infection. Sam knew that wild animal scratches could be very dangerous, even deadly, if they got this bad. If the infection got into his blood, he might not live—even if he and Sara were rescued today.

Sam tried to calm himself down and think. What could he do? He didn't know enough about plants to have any idea what might draw out or kill bacteria. Once, he had read that beeswax was good to put on cuts and scratches, but he wasn't about to go tearing apart a honeycomb even if he could find one. At home, he might put antiseptic or rubbing alcohol on a scratch, but . . . That was it!

Sam picked up his backpack and tiptoed out of the cave. It was just getting light. He did the best he could to wash the scratches off with one of the cups of water. Then he dug out Sara's bottle of hand sanitizer and read the ingredients. There was a lot of stuff he'd never heard of, but the first ingredient listed was alcohol. That meant there was a lot of it in the sanitizer. Sam took a deep breath and poured some on the infected scratches. The sharp stinging nearly took his breath away, and his eyes watered. But Sam emptied the bottle and let the alcohol seep in.

I'm in the middle of nowhere at 6 a.m. pouring Handy Dandy on my arm, Sam thought in an attempt to get his mind off the pain. But even his humor wasn't helping now. The pain was twice as bad as when the bear had actually clawed him. He closed his eyes and allowed a few tears to roll down his face. Then he shook his head and waited. Finally, the searing burning began fading. Sam took the last trash bag and wrapped it around his arm, and then he took Sara's elastic hair ties and moved them up his arm to hold the bag in place. Then he sat on a rock, shivering and waiting for the sun to come up and the pain to die down.

As the woods around him awoke, Sam heard a lot of bird chattering and commotion a bit further down the hill. Sam watched dozens of birds fly in. They were all eagerly eating something that was growing on a wide patch of scraggly bushes. Curious, Sam wandered down the hill to get a closer look. Fat, dark berries covered the bushes and lay in heaps on the ground. Excitedly, Sam hurried over, scattering the startled birds everywhere. Blackberries! Or, at least, they smelled and looked like blackberries. Sam cautiously bit into one. It was a little tart, but the fruity taste was delicious—particularly after not eating anything for nearly two days.

It wasn't easy collecting berries with only one good arm, but Sam loaded as many as he could into a pouch in his backpack. And as he picked berries, he thought hard. Today was the day he and Sara *must* get rescued. There was no question about it. Thirty minutes later, Sam headed back to the cave. Not only did he have breakfast—he also had a plan.

CHAPTER 12

"But I thought we needed to be on top of the mountain for them to see us," Sara said between mouthfuls of berries. She had eaten so many that her face and hands were purple. Both she and Sam were so hungry that the berries tasted like candy.

"We can't waste another day just waiting up there," Sam explained. "And I know for a fact that Lake Crystal is down in the valley. I saw it through binoculars. If we can get down to the lake, we can find help."

Sara didn't look completely convinced.

"Look," Sam continued, digging for the last of the berries. "There are roads to the lake, a marina, lots of people out on boats, and even a park. We'd have to be invisible for nobody to see us! Plus, it's Thursday."

Sara stared at Sam blankly. "What's that have to do with anything?"

"Everyone from Camp Crystal is headed to the lake," Sam said. "If we head there too, it increases our chances of being found."

"You really think they're still having camp?" Sara asked doubtfully. "I mean, after we've disappeared? They probably sent everyone home."

"Oh, true," Sam said. Somehow that hadn't occurred to him. Now he understood why they had heard the dinner bell only once. Camp Crystal had shut down. This realization made him feel worse. Nothing like ruining vacation for 60 kids from your own small town. It was going to be a long school year.

"What if we get lost?" Sara asked, snapping Sam back from his glum thoughts.

"We won't," Sam replied. "I've got a plan for that, too."

Sam reached into the backpack and pulled out the Camp Crystal itinerary. It was a little damp and stained with blackberries, but otherwise, it was in good shape.

"As we walk down the hill, we'll leave parts of pages from this about every 50 yards. This paper's bright yellow—there's no way we can miss it," Sam explained. "So, if we can't find the lake, we'll just follow the paper trail back here. At least we know where the ridge is from this spot, and we know there's food and shelter here."

Sara looked truly impressed.

"And there's an added bonus," Sam said modestly. "If anyone searching for us comes across *any* of those pieces of paper, they'll know they're on the right track. Most of the trained rescuers will understand that we're leaving a trail for them to follow."

"Wow," Sara almost whispered. "Maybe they *will* find us today."

Sam just shook his head. "There's no 'maybe.' They're definitely going to find us. They have to."

For the next few hours, they made their way down the mountain, leaving bright pieces of paper on trees and bushes. It was a beautiful late-summer day, and Sam and Sara were so revived by sleep, water, food, and hope, that they actually laughed and told a few bad jokes. But by early afternoon, the laughter had died down. Completely.

"We're almost out of paper," Sam murmured with a confused look. Somehow, it hadn't occurred to him that they wouldn't have reached the lake by the time the pages ran out. "But we're no longer going downhill. I don't get it . . . the lake must be right around here. I saw it through the binoculars."

Worse than this, however, were the strange pulsating pains in Sam's arm and the horrible bouts of dizziness that forced him to grasp at branches to keep from losing his balance. The edges of his vision were slowly blurring, and spots of bright color and light kept dancing in front of him. And then the heat—Sam felt as though the backs of his eyes were on fire and the fire was slowly spilling through his entire body. Thirst came raging back far worse than at any other point in the past two days.

The infection, Sam thought miserably. *So the sanitizer didn't work, after all. No big surprise.*

Finally, Sam just stumbled to the ground and sat awkwardly on his knees.

"I . . . I just need to rest a second," Sam gasped. He leaned forward, trying to stop the spinning of the ground.

Sara immediately slumped next to her brother and grabbed her stomach.

"Me too," she groaned. "I didn't want to say anything, but . . . "

"What?" Sam said, alarmed. He stared at his sister. Her face was very pale, and she was sweating even though there was a cool breeze. "What's wrong with you? I thought I felt like this because of an infection in my arm."

"My stomach," Sara said weakly. "I keep getting sharp pains, and I feel kind of sick. And I'm so thirsty."

The berries! Sam had been so sure that they were blackberries, but what if they weren't? What if he had accidentally poisoned both of them? If they couldn't keep moving, his and Sara's odds of getting rescued would go way down. And if they collapsed out here in the middle of nowhere . . . Sam couldn't bear to think about it. Slowly, he pulled himself up. Then he helped Sara lean on her walking stick, and they began walking again very slowly. Just beyond a stand of hemlocks, the trees seemed to thin out a little. Maybe the lake was just past that.

At that moment, the unmistakable sound of a helicopter in the distance drifted through the forest.

"No!" Sam shouted in frustration. There was no time to create another distress signal, and he and Sara were still too covered by trees to be seen. If they could just get to where the trees were not so thick . . . But now the helicopter hummed closer. Sam could tell it was hovering and searching for them. Sam fought the dizziness and waves of heat that were beginning to overwhelm him as his mind raced. There had to be *something* he and Sara could do to be seen!

Suddenly, Sam remembered the last thing in the backpack—Sara's mirror. Sam knew that if a mirror catches the sun just right, it can send a bright signal to someone in a plane or helicopter. A lot of hikers carry special signal mirrors with sight holes in them that make it easier to focus on a plane. Three quick flashes of light to a pilot indicate that help is needed. It wouldn't be nearly as easy trying to focus Sara's little pink-handled mirror, but Sam would have to try.

"We have to get to that opening," Sam said to Sara, as he dug the mirror out of the backpack. About 100 yards away was what looked like a small clearing. The chopping sound of the helicopter was getting sharper. But now Sara fell to the ground and just shook her head.

"I can't," she mumbled. "Too sick."

Sam knelt next to Sara for only a moment and brushed the hair off her soaked forehead.

"Don't worry. I'll signal with the mirror and let them know we're here, and then I'll be right back. Then someone will be here to rescue us. I promise."

Sara barely nodded, and then she doubled over and threw up purple berries everywhere.

Whoosh, whoosh, whoosh.

The helicopter was closing in. Sam took one last worried look at Sara and then staggered toward the clearing, gripping the mirror in his shaking hand. Only fifty more yards.

Whoosh, whoosh, whoosh.

Now everything seemed to be tilting and moving. Sparks of light and darkness were making it hard for Sam to focus on anything, much less three flashes of light to someone 1,000 feet overhead. *Just ahead of that tree*, Sam thought, as he struggled to remain upright. His whole body was cramping, and he was nearly bent in half. A piercing ringing was filling his ears. Just as he reached the edge of where the trees cleared a bit, Sam's strength ended. It felt as though a door had suddenly been slammed in his face.

In one last desperate attempt, Sam lifted the mirror up awkwardly toward the sky and the approaching helicopter. But dizziness overcame him in a massive wave. The mirror flew out of his hand and shattered into a dozen pieces against a rock.

"No!" Sam gasped. In a hazy blur, Sam saw the helicopter between gaps in the trees. It passed directly overhead, paused in a hover, and then seemed ready to move on. "Wait! Help!" Sam tried to shout, but it was barely louder than a choked rasp. Sam crawled out into the clearing on his hands and knees. The sound of his heart pounding and his gasping for air were nearly drowning out the hovering helicopter. Slowly, fuzzy darkness began closing in.

Then—Sam felt a firm hand on his shoulder.

A hiker carrying a tattered backpack and a hiking stick was standing above him. Sam tried to sit up and speak, but the man eased him back down to the ground gently.

"It's all right now," the man said in a distant, watery voice. "I'm getting help for you."

Sam stared up at the man for only a moment. The man's face was old, but his eyes were kind and bright—very bright. As Sam began losing consciousness, the brightness of the stranger's eyes looked like they were mixing with the sparks of light that kept swirling all around him. Slowly, the stranger seemed to be drifting away like a dream. Then everything went dark.

CHAPTER 13

"It's really pretty amazing that they survived two nights out in that rain and then the cold with not much more than trash bags."

"And no food or shelter either. I can't imagine how they did it."

"Well, they should have quite a story to tell once they feel up to it."

Sam kept hearing voices drift in and out. It was like someone was talking at the end of a long hallway. Then the voices began getting clearer, and Sam came out of a half-dream about trees and dirt and rain and blood. He felt a strange hollow feeling in his stomach. Then his eyes fluttered open.

"Sam! You're awake!"

Sam's mother was leaning over him, smiling, with tears streaming down her face at the same time. A serious-looking man in a white coat stood next to her.

"Um . . . ," Sam mumbled as he focused his eyes. "Where am I?"

He was in a strange room with three tubes coming out of his right arm. His left arm was covered in clean white bandages. Sam tried moving it and immediately decided that was not a good idea.

"Honey, you're in the hospital," his mother said. "But you're going to be fine, and we're all just so—"

"Sara?" Sam suddenly interrupted. A sketchy memory of the moment right before he passed out came flooding back. He had left Sara collapsed and poisoned back in the woods. The hiker stranger said he'd get help, but had he even seen Sara?

"Your sister is still sleeping," said the man in the white coat. As the man smiled at him, Sam realized he must be a doctor. "She has only a little bacterial sickness from the water you two must have drunk. And, of course, she's very tired."

"Uncle Joe is down the hall in her room," Sam's mother explained.

"So the berries . . . ," Sam said weakly, "they . . . they didn't kill her?"

Sam's mother and the doctor looked at each other.

"Well, if you two ate some berries you found in the woods, you picked the right ones," the doctor said. "Nobody's dying, but you have a pretty nasty infection in that arm. That made you a lot sicker than the water. An animal scratch?"

Sam sighed with relief about Sara. How long had he been asleep? He suddenly felt incredibly hungry. Did they have cheeseburgers in this hospital? What about chips?

"What caused it? An animal?" the doctor asked again about the scratch.

"Oh, yeah," Sam said absently, thinking about ice cream. "A bear."

"A *what*?"

Uncle Joe had just walked in the room. He went over to Sam and put both his arms around him and gave him a long hug, while Sam's mother held Sam's hand tightly and cried a little more. Sam was just beginning to feel awkward when Uncle Joe stood up and cleared his throat.

"So, you're going to have to tell us all about everything before and after this bear incident as soon as your strength is back."

Sam looked at his uncle and mother and managed a small grin.

"I think a banana split would give me a lot of strength."

The doctor smiled, gently but firmly. He wouldn't let him have cheeseburgers or ice cream yet. But the chicken soup, something Sam usually didn't like, was incredible.

He was on his third bowl as he neared the end of his story. "And that's when Sara got sick and I started passing out."

"But not before you signaled the pilot," Uncle Joe said.

"What?" Sam asked blankly. "I never signaled anyone. The mirror broke before I had a chance. It was that hiker that got us help at the lake. I guess he had a signal mirror with him. Who is he, anyway? I definitely want to thank him."

Now Uncle Joe looked confused.

"Sam, there was no one else there," his mother said quietly. "When they brought the helicopter down, it was just you and Sara. The rescue pilot was amazed that you had been able to signal him with three flashes that bright—particularly in your condition."

Sam shook his head. "No, seriously. Who was that guy? He must have followed the pieces of paper we left on the trees. I guess we were near a hiking trail, after all. The last thing he said was that he was going to get help."

Sam's mother put her hand on Sam's forehead to see if he was still running a fever. It had gotten as high as 104.

"I think you must have imagined that, buddy," Uncle Joe said. "You and Sara were more than eight miles away from any trails, and the lake was even a couple miles farther away than that. Sometimes high fevers can make you see things."

"But I . . . the mirror broke . . . that hiker . . ." Sam stammered in confusion. "I wasn't imagining anything. At least, I don't think I was."

Sam's mother smiled and smoothed his hair.

"None of that matters, really," she said. "As long as you're safe, everything's okay."

"Well, it matters a little bit," Uncle Joe said with a wink, "because a writer from *Real Survival* magazine called and asked if you'd be willing to tell them your story for their next issue."

Sam's eyes grew wide. "No way! Really?"

"Yep, really," Uncle Joe said. "They're doing a series called 'The Bravest Teens,' and they want to include you."

The bravest, Sam thought. It made him feel a little funny. No one had ever referred to him as brave before, and certainly not as the bravest.

"When?" Sam asked.

"As soon as you're up to it," Uncle Joe replied. "But you should wait a few days until you feel stronger. Maybe things will be clearer to you then."

Sam and Sara came home the next day, and Uncle Joe's doorbell rang constantly. Suddenly, the brother and sister who had survived all alone in the mountains were big stars. They had made news from coast to coast. And in the small town of Blueville, they were instant celebrities.

Pete, Jake, and Darnell came by and wanted to see the bear scratch.

"Man, you fought a *bear*!" Jake said. "With your hands!"

"Well, not exactly," Sam said. But everyone who heard Sam and Sara's story refused to believe anything less than the fact that Sam was a hero.

Even Deanna and two of her friends came

by to drop off some cookies and stare shyly at Sam. When Sam told them about using Sara's big pink hair ties to secure a trash bag to his arm, they laughed like it was the funniest thing they'd ever heard.

"So, will you sign my copy of *Real Survival* when it comes out?" Deanna asked with her wide smile.

Sam just blushed and nodded.

Finally, when the flurry of visitors and news reporters died down, Sam and Sara had some time to be alone and talk about what they'd been through. Late one afternoon, the two of them sat out on the swing on the front porch. The writer from *Real Survival* would be coming the next day, so Sam was trying to get his facts straight.

"You're absolutely positive you didn't see that hiker when they rescued us?" Sam asked for the tenth time. "I mean, you were conscious—I wasn't."

"Positive. Again," Sara said with a sigh. "I could see you near the clearing. First you fell down, then there were those flashes of light from my mirror, and about five minutes later, the helicopter landed. There was no one else there."

Sam shook his head. Maybe he *had* imagined it. After all, high fevers can make you kind of crazy. People often see things that aren't there when their bodies are under extreme stress. Sam decided he would just tell the magazine writer that he tried to use the mirror, it broke, and everything was a blur after that. That was pretty much the truth anyway, right?

Just then, a delivery truck rumbled along the street. It made Sam think briefly of Bart and Alex and the loud Jeep. It occurred to him that he hadn't thought of them in days. It also occurred to him that the thought of them no longer scared him. Three days lost in the mountains that included a run-in with a bear, bats, killer lightning, hunger, sickness, terror, and pain—after that, a couple of loudmouthed bullies didn't seem all that frightening.

"Hey, I haven't seen Bart roaring his Jeep up and down the street since we got back," Sam said. "Not that I miss it."

"Oh, those idiots," Sara said, rolling her eyes. "You didn't hear about them?"

Sam just shook his head.

"Vicky told me they're both in big trouble. They were the ones scaring everyone up at the camp that first night. Alex got kicked off the football team, and Bart's grounded for, like, forever."

"How'd they get caught?" Sam asked. He remembered hearing the Jeep heading back down the mountain. He was certain they had gotten away with their prank.

"They were drinking beer and drove off the road and into a tree down by Crystal Lake. When the cops got there, they found the beard and cane and stuff in the backseat. Shirley had just put in a call to the police, so it wasn't very hard to figure out."

"Wow," Sam said quietly. "They weren't hurt, were they?"

"No. They just put a couple dents in the Jeep. But I guess they were pretty embarrassed about getting in an accident. They kept trying to blame it on some guy who they said was crossing the road. Bart said he had to swerve to miss him."

"A guy crossing the road?" Sam asked. "In the middle of the night?"

"I know. What a lame lie, right?" Sara snorted. "Bart complained to the cops that it wasn't his fault, but the cops just ignored him."

Sam looked at his sister and felt his heart skip a beat.

"Did they say anything else about him—like what he looked like?" Sam asked carefully.

Sara thought for a moment.

"Not really. Just some old hiker guy with a backpack."

CHAPTER 14

"So you say you were rescued by a ghost, eh?" the writer from *Real Survival* said with a grin. "That's definitely a first. Are you sure that's what you want to say? Or, rather, are you sure that's what happened?"

Sam just smiled and nodded. He'd been up half the night thinking about it, but he finally figured it out. When he and Pete were looking at Crystal Lake through the binoculars on that first day at camp, Pete mentioned that Old Man Smith's property had been about ten miles west of the lake. That was exactly where Sam and Sara had been rescued.

And hadn't the camp counselor told a story about Old Man Smith's ghost raising his cane and disappearing after a blinding flash of light? Sam was positive that Sara's mirror had broken before he could catch the sunlight on it even once. He hadn't signaled the helicopter—the ghost of Old Man Smith had. What looked like a hiking stick must have been his cane. Sam couldn't figure out why the ghost didn't have a long beard or why Sara hadn't seen it. Most of all, Sam couldn't understand why Old Man Smith decided to help him. But it was just like the counselor with the dragon tattoos had said that first night—who really understands ghosts, anyway?

Sam never told anyone, not even Sara, that he was certain that the hiker Bart and Alex had swerved to miss was the ghost of Old Man Smith. As it turned out, the boys had crashed not too far from where Sam and Sara had been rescued: Old Man Smith's haunting territory near his land. It kind of bothered Sam that the ghost hadn't done something worse to Bart and Alex. A couple of dents in the Jeep didn't seem like much of a revenge on bullies. Old Man Smith could have at least banged those two jerks over the head with his cane or something.

So why did Old Man Smith help me, anyway? Sam continued to wonder. *I thought he haunted the mountains looking for revenge, not for lost campers.*

Sam got his answer later that fall.

"I could never have been that brave out there," Deanna said quietly.

Sam and Deanna were looking out over the mountain valley where Sam and Sara had wandered, lost, for nearly three days. It was a beautiful fall day, and Uncle Joe had brought the family up to the mountains near Camp Crystal for a picnic. Sam had asked Deanna to come along. His first few weeks at Washington High had been way better than he ever would have imagined. Pete, Jake, and Darnell were becoming really good friends—and not just because Sam was a local hero. They liked Sam because he was funny and honest and thoughtful.

And now Sam even had a girlfriend.

← I think his gf is Deanna

"You know, I've never really thought of myself as brave," Sam explained to Deanna. "I mean, I've always been too small to fight back if . . . well, if someone picks on me."

Deanna looked at Sam in surprise. "Fighting back doesn't mean you're brave. It just means you're doing the same thing that the person who's picking on you is doing. Being brave is what you did down there. You put yourself second and took care of your sister first."

← Deanna saying that what Sam did for his sister was great.

Sam looked doubtful and shrugged. "Yeah . . . well . . . ," he began. Then he decided to confide in Deanna. He told her all about Bart and Alex and how they had pushed him around and hit him and how he couldn't fight back.

"If only I were bigger," Sam concluded with a frown, "I could get back at them big time."

"Bart and Alex are stupid," Deanna said with a huff. "They used to do the same sort of things to my brother, Adam."

"Your brother!" Sam said in amazement. "But Adam's the quarterback. And really big."

"Yeah, well, Adam stutters when he gets nervous. So Alex and Bart used to push him around all the time and make fun of him," Deanna explained. "It has nothing to do with your being small. Those guys just like to pick on anyone who's different. That's what bullies do."

"But they don't bother him now," Sam said. "Did he finally punch them out and scare them off?"

"Hardly!" Deanna said with a laugh. "Adam's never hit anyone."

"Then how did he get rid of them?" Sam asked, confused.

Deanna just shrugged. "It wasn't so much that he *did* anything to them. But he made new friends, and then he found out he was really good at football. He's a pretty happy person, and people like him. Once Bart and Alex realized that, I guess picking on him wasn't as much fun anymore."

Sam thought about this for a while, as a shower of bright red leaves swept through the woods.

"In our English class last week," Deanna finally said, "Ms. Taylor read a quote by some ancient guy who had said, 'Happiness is the best revenge.' I guess that's my point, if you know what I mean."

Those words were like a bell ringing, waking Sam up. Suddenly, everything became very clear to him. Bart and Alex had continued to call him names and shove him in the hallways when school first began, but lately they were paying less and less attention to him. *Because I'm happy*, Sam thought, as he shyly reached for Deanna's hand. *Really happy*.

The best revenge. Now Sam understood why Old Man Smith had helped him. In the end, Sam's happiness was the best way to pay back a couple of modern-day bullies. It seems the old ghost had learned a thing or two about bullies over the past 100 years.

"You know what?" Sam said with a smile. "I don't think anyone will ever see the ghost of Old Man Smith again. He's gone for good."

Deanna looked questioningly at Sam and squeezed his hand. But Sam was looking out over the valley near Crystal Lake. Then he gazed up at the towering mountains. Sam was already looking forward to hiking in them again next summer. He realized that he had no more fear of the wilderness surrounding him, only awe and respect. It was a really good feeling. But even better than this was a most unusual feeling that made Sam grin up at the sky.

For the first time in his life, Sam felt about ten feet tall.

♡ 100% ♡

I like this book!

♡ 100% ♡

I juss
LOVE IT